D0239692

Incident at
Pegasus Heights

When fossil-hunter Jim Dragon is on his way to Bear Creek to sell his latest discovery, he goes to the aid of a woman in distress, Elmina Fay. Unfortunately, Pierre Dulaine takes advantage of the situation and steals his fossils.

Jim vows to reclaim his property and Elmina offers to help him, but only if he'll do something for her. She has heard a tale about the bones of a winged horse being found nearby and she wants Jim to find Pegasus' remains for her.

At first, Jim is sceptical about embarking on such a mission, but before long he discovers that the truth behind the tale is even stranger than he could ever have imagined.

Incident at Pegasus Heights

I.J. Parnham

A Black Horse Western

ROBERT HALE

1076427/ALF

© I.J. Parnham 2017
First published in Great Britain 2017

ISBN 978-0-7198-2162-2

The Crowood Press
The Stable Block
Crowood Lane
Ramsbury
Marlborough
Wiltshire SN8 2HR

www.bhwesterns.com

Robert Hale is an imprint
of The Crowood Press

The right of I.J. Parnham to be identified as
author of this work has been asserted by him
in accordance with the Copyright, Designs and
Patents Act 1988

Typeset by
Derek Doyle & Associates, Shaw Heath
Printed and bound in Great Britain by
CPI Group (UK) Ltd, Croydon, CR0 4YY

CHAPTER 1

The woman was heading for trouble.

For the last hour Jim Dragon had been lying on his belly in a depression watching the two men who were loitering beside the trail.

These men had done nothing other than lean back against a boulder and look away from the town of Beaver Ridge, presumably as they waited for him. Their irritated postures and frequent angry exchanges of views had made Jim hope they'd move on soon, but the woman's arrival had caught their interest.

She was walking slowly. Every few paces she stopped to raise a foot so she could look at the sole, presumably because her small boots made her feel every stone on the trail.

Her dark clothing and lack of headwear were unsuitable for the high sun and the carpetbag she clutched in both hands was too bulky for a long journey.

Yet Beaver Ridge was ten miles away and there

were no settlements behind her for at least a day's ride. Jim wondered how he'd passed her on the way here without noticing her when the men spoke up.

'Now, what do we have here?' one man asked, stepping forward.

The woman stopped and dropped the bag to the ground with a thud. She wiped sweat from her cheeks and neck, fluffed her fair hair, and put a hand to her brow to shield her eyes from the sun.

Despite the obvious danger she faced, she provided a cheery wave that made both men glance at each other and smirk before they moved on to meet her. Their way took them past the hollow where Jim was hiding and so he hugged the ground until their footfalls had gone by.

'I'm Elmina Fay,' she said, her voice light and unconcerned. 'Would you men be so kind as to help me get to town? I'm awful weary.'

'We sure would like to help, but we're kind of busy right now,' one man said. 'What have you got to offer to change our minds?'

Jim raised himself to find the men were twenty yards away and they were behaving as he'd expected. They had their backs to him and they were standing with their hands on their hips blocking her path.

Although she still appeared calm, Jim got to his knees and crawled forward to the lip of the depression.

'I can pay you for your trouble,' Elmina said.

'How much have you got?' the second man asked.

Elmina knelt and opened up her bag.

'I'll pay both of you a dollar to get me—'

'I didn't ask that.' The man lowered his tone and advanced a pace. 'I asked how much you had?'

Elmina flinched, as if becoming aware for the first time of the likely direction this encounter would take. Then, becoming flustered, she rummaged around in her bag while the men stood over her and cast amused glances at each other.

That sight was enough for Jim. He was packing a six-shooter, as were both the men, and so when he stood up, he walked quietly towards them.

Elmina still had her head lowered as she searched. Her slowness in finding money made one man grunt in irritation while the other man bent over to snatch the bag away from her.

His hand had yet to reach the bag when he jerked aside quickly. The second man took a step backwards giving Jim an uninterrupted view of Elmina and the pistol she had whipped out of the bag.

'Now, how much money have you got?' she said with a grin.

Her grin died when she saw Jim. She swung the gun towards him making Jim halt. He shook his head and raised his hands.

His reaction made her narrow her eyes, presumably in confusion about what his intentions were and, with her attention on him, the two men took advantage.

One man kicked the bag knocking it into her legs and unbalancing her, while the second man lunged forward and grabbed her arm. He thrust her arm up

7

high with ease and with a deft twist of the wrist he made her drop the pistol.

In moments, he held her from behind while the second man turned a gun on Jim. He provided a mocking tip of the hat and then waggled a warning finger.

'Much obliged,' he said.

Jim couldn't think of an appropriate reply and so he fingered the lucky shark's tooth he wore around his neck. As he remained still, Elmina tried to tear herself free.

She squirmed and kicked her captor, but that only encouraged him to hold her more tightly. Then he raised her from the ground and walked her to the boulder where the men had been waiting.

'Let me go,' she demanded, glaring at Jim as she was moved past him.

'You've got me wrong,' Jim said, backing away for a pace. 'I came to help you.'

'Help me?' she spluttered. 'I was doing fine until you arrived!'

Jim couldn't argue with this and his irritated expression made her captors laugh.

While one man held her securely in the shade of the boulder, the second man walked up to him. He held out his left hand while aiming the gun in his right hand at Jim's chest.

Jim handed over his six-shooter and when he joined Elmina beside the boulder, she directed her ire at him with a harsh glare and clenched fists.

'I know that now,' he said with a weary air. 'But

believe me, in the end you'll be glad I came.'

'Why?'

'Because these men were waiting for me and that means they'll get more entertainment from capturing me than they would from tormenting you.'

She acknowledged his point with a brief nod. Then she looked back along the route she'd taken to get here.

Reinforcing Jim's statement, three riders were now coming along the trail towards them. In the far distance, a wagon was also approaching.

She stopped struggling, seemingly accepting her best chance of getting out of the situation relatively unscathed was not to draw attention to herself.

Nobody spoke again until the lead rider drew up before them. He considered Elmina with surprise before he leaned down to grin at Jim.

'And so we meet again, Monsieur Dragon,' the newcomer announced.

'I always look forward to our meetings, Pierre Dulaine,' Jim said.

'I don't believe you're being entirely honest after you led me such a merry chase, but it was not merry enough, I fear.' Pierre looked over his shoulder at the wagon. 'Your careful plans are now unravelling.'

'You'll never defeat all my plans.'

Jim fingered his shark's tooth, making Pierre laugh.

'That boast failed to chill my blood. I know you touch that tooth when you've accepted you're in a dire situation and your only hope is to get a lucky break.'

Jim lowered his hand, making Pierre chuckle before he looked at Elmina; her presence was an unexpected element to the conclusion of their chase and it made him frown.

'Jim's luck has deserted him,' one of the captors said. 'He was sneaking up on us and he might have surprised us, but this woman came walking down the trail and he tried to help her.'

'He didn't help nothing!' Elmina shouted, but her interjection only made Pierre point at her.

'Hold her securely,' he said, 'Jim's a cunning devil and he is famed for his carefully laid traps. She'll be a part of his plans.'

'I've never seen that idiot before,' Elmina spluttered. 'And I never want to see him again.'

She opened her mouth to pour more scorn on Jim and his actions. Then she lowered her head in acceptance of the fact that the more she complained, the more likely it appeared that she was, in fact, working with Jim.

Her reaction killed off Jim's theory that she was working for Pierre – he accepted that her arrival had been bad luck.

'Tell her what you were doing, Monsieur Dragon,' Pierre said. 'That should make her rest easy while we wait for your wagon to arrive.'

Dulaine's sceptical tone showed he still believed Jim was working with her. Dragon felt that Pierre's uncertainty might give him an opportunity to escape, so he related a fairly accurate version of his life story. His explanation made her look at him with interest

10

for the first time.

He was a bone-hunter. He tracked down and dug up the huge bones of long dead lizards, a talent he had honed over the last decade. Then he sold the fossils to men who were prepared to pay handsomely for the chance to study them or just for the privilege of owning an unusual artefact.

Jim wasn't interested in their reason for wanting the bones. His motivation was to test himself with the challenge of the quest. The money helped, too.

'I've heard tales about men like you,' she said when he'd finished, her tone less irritated than before. 'I assume Jim Dragon isn't your real name.'

'I have an interesting story to tell about that, too,' Jim said.

'I've heard it before and it's very dull,' Pierre said with an exaggerated yawn. 'Although, now that you've failed, I'd welcome hearing how you planned to get past me.'

Jim scowled. Although he had a skill for sniffing out dinosaur bones, finding them was only half the battle.

He then had to get them to the men who would pay him. That put him in danger of encountering men like Pierre, who didn't have an ability to find bones, but who could sniff out men like Jim. But Jim was resourceful and so he'd got wind of the fact Pierre was following him.

He'd hidden his wagon, loaded down with his latest discovery. Then he'd sneaked away and sought out the men who were pursuing him.

As his wagon was now being brought to a halt, that precaution appeared to have failed even before the confusion caused by Elmina's unexpected arrival.

Pierre questioned the driver – whom he identified as Nicholson – about where he'd found the wagon. Then he ordered two men to climb on to the back to examine the contents of the two crates stored there.

As this process took a while, Elmina's captors released her and stood to either side of Jim.

With their attention redirected, Elmina fetched her bag and sat with it clutched to her chest. Pierre wasn't adept at identifying fossils and so he moved his horse on to look down at her.

'Can I go now?' she said. 'It's a long walk to town and it'll be sundown in a few hours.'

'When I've confirmed that Monsieur Dragon hasn't played one of his famous tricks on me such as filling the crates with rocks and hiding the real bones elsewhere, I'd be delighted if you'd accompanied me to town.'

Pierre gave a short bow and fingered his trim moustache.

'If I have to choose between an arrogant Frenchman and an idiot,' she said, 'I'd sooner stay with the idiot.'

Her comment made Nicholson laugh and so, while barking orders, Pierre headed to the wagon.

He consulted the men who were examining the crates. This involved plenty of shrugging and lots of pointing at the items in the crates until an obvious bone caught Pierre's attention.

His observations helped Pierre regain his good humour and he beckoned everyone to move out.

When the riders had mounted and the other men were on the wagon, Pierre moved his horse on to loom over Jim for a final gloat.

'It would appear that this time I'll enjoy the spoils of your months of hard work,' he declared, 'while all you'll enjoy is your blisters and your aching back.'

'That would appear to be the case, but don't be so sure,' Jim said slowly, hoping to encourage Pierre's doubts, but Pierre merely grinned as the wagon moved past him.

'Happy digging in the future, Monsieur Dragon. I hope your luck returns, so you can again furnish me with riches without my having to soil my hands.'

Jim didn't respond and so with a final grin, Pierre rode off. Elmina watched him head away and then leaned towards Jim.

'So have you hidden the real bones somewhere else, then?' she said as Jim glared at Pierre's back.

'Nope,' Jim said.

'Then you've played some kind of trick on him?'

'Nope.'

She considered him with mounting exasperation.

'So you're just going to stand there and let him ride off with your property, are you?'

'Sure.'

She shook her bag at him. 'Fine rescuer you turned out to be.'

'And a fine woman in distress you turned out to be.'

13

He fingered his shark's tooth while he watched the wagon with his horses and his property move on, their slow pace serving to taunt him.

With a weary sigh she threw the bag down at his feet. Jim ignored the hint and stepped over the bag before he moved on, making her grab the bag and scurry along to catch up with him.

'So what you're saying is: Pierre won and you lost and you don't have a single plan in mind to reclaim your property other than to trust you'll get lucky?'

Jim could muster only a shrug and so she hefted the bag over a shoulder. Then she broke into a run while yelling at Pierre to wait for her.

After trundling on for a dozen yards, the wagon stopped and Pierre jumped down from his horse.

When she reached him, they spoke briefly before he helped her up on to the back of the wagon while offering several deep bows. Then he swapped positions with one of his men and joined her.

'I reckon my luck won't change,' Jim said to himself as she directed a cheery wave at him. 'But I reckon Pierre's luck is about to run out.'

CHAPTER 2

'So what's a charming lady like you doing out here all alone?' Pierre Dulaine said.

'I'm sitting on the back of your wagon listening to your prattle,' Elmina said.

Nicholson Perry, the driver, laughed, making Pierre glare at him before he turned back to Elmina.

'But you must be tired and hungry, Madam Fay. I intend to rest up for an hour in Beaver Ridge.' Pierre fingered his moustache. 'Perhaps you'd like to accompany me to dinner.'

'If you want to buy me a meal, I'll eat it, but I won't be moving on anywhere with you, or doing anything else with you either.'

'I hope you will change your mind. I'm a courteous and generous man, and thanks to Monsieur Dragon, I'm now a wealthy man.'

With a determined movement she fixed her gaze on the approaching town making Pierre chuckle. Then he sat back confidently, as if that had been his first ploy in a game he was sure he'd win.

Pierre's attitude made Nicholson even more depressed than he had been already. The prospect of visiting Beaver Ridge for the first time in three months had been bad enough, and the incident with Jim Dragon hadn't helped.

'Give up before you make a fool of yourself, Pierre,' he said when the wagon reached the outskirts of town. 'Your charm's not working on her.'

'I'm not interested in your opinion,' Pierre said.

Nicholson gripped the reins tightly. 'That won't stop me from giving it to you. You lied. We didn't reclaim your property. We stole something that was never yours in the first place.'

'So you believed me!'

Pierre barked out a peel of laughter and then looked around for someone to share his amusement. Elmina ignored him and the riders were looking ahead, but when they drew up outside a saloon, Pierre was still smiling.

Pierre gave everyone instructions. They were to eat and stock up on provisions before they moved on to Bear Creek. He hoped to leave before Jim Dragon arrived.

Pierre ordered Nicholson to guard the crates, but Nicholson jumped down from the wagon. Then he set off down the main drag.

Pierre called after him, but he didn't look back, even when he heard laughter.

He headed to the opposite side of town where Beaver Ridge jail cast a gloomy shadow over the buildings. He considered the formidable structure, but it didn't make him feel any better about returning to town.

Four months ago, Nicholson and his friend Grantham Fletcher had arrived in town looking for work. The only job they had been offered was working as temporary deputies for the town marshal Bradley Collier.

Apparently, the outlaw Chadwick Jackson had carried out a string of raids against the Pegasus Lumber Company. The owner of the company, Winslow Scott, was demanding action and so one of his guards, Murdock Lark, had vowed to find Chadwick.

Bearing in mind Murdock's brutal methods, Marshal Collier was determined to get to Chadwick first, and he had tasked Nicholson and Grantham with finding him.

After a month of fruitless searching, the two deputies had failed to make progress, and so they decided to stop looking for Chadwick and follow Murdock instead.

Sure enough, Murdock's movements had been odd; they had followed him to an abandoned and rat-infested homestead. Chadwick wasn't there, but they found property that had been stolen from the lumber company.

Murdock had refused to explain himself and so they had arrested him. Later, Murdock was found guilty of being in possession of the stolen property, although it couldn't be proved that he had helped Chadwick carry out the raids.

When Murdock had been sentenced to a year in Beaver Ridge jail, he had blamed his capture on Nicholson and Grantham, and he had vowed that when he came out, he would make them suffer.

As Chadwick's raids had stopped, both Winslow Scott and Marshal Collier had been satisfied with how things had turned out, but with their task completed Nicholson and Grantham were left looking for work again. Grantham had found work at a mercantile in town, but Nicholson had decided that he should move on.

Unfortunately, that decision had led to him working for Pierre and now he was back in Beaver Ridge.

He headed to the nearest saloon where he ordered some coffee and sat in the darkest corner. Through a grimy window he watched the low sunlight play across the jail. He resolved not to leave until the sunlight reddened, as by then he'd be sure that Pierre had moved on without him.

As it was, a few minutes later a familiar voice spoke up.

'Howdy, Nicholson.'

He looked up to see a face that was as grim-set as his own must be, and the half-empty whiskey bottle dangling from the hand of his friend Grantham Fletcher suggested he'd been in the saloon for a while.

Nicholson pushed out a chair and Grantham fetched a clean glass before he joined him. When Grantham nudged Nicholson's coffee mug aside and placed the empty glass before him, Nicholson shook his head.

'Liquor doesn't solve nothing,' he said.

'I know,' Grantham said, 'but when you've had a day like the one I've had, it's the only option.'

'Nothing ever changes for us, does it?' Nicholson sighed. Then he filled his glass and topped up Grantham's. 'Let's see who's had the worst day. The winner gets the satisfaction of knowing someone else is worse off than he is.'

The two men snorted harsh laughs. Grantham clinked his glass against Nicholson's and leaned forward, the challenge making his eyes gleam.

'I lost someone's property and I lost my job.'

Nicholson shrugged. 'I stole someone's property and I lost my job.'   1 0 76 ⊂2 7 1 ALF

Grantham winced. 'You win, although you don't look like a man with money.'

'I'm not. I've been working for this no-account varmint Pierre Dulaine who was looking for a Jim Dragon. They have history, so I didn't ask questions.' Nicholson sipped his whiskey. 'Today, we found Jim and stole everything he had, except now that I think about it, I reckon Jim was in the right.'

'What are you going to do about it?'

'Drink with you until Pierre's left town.' He swirled his drink, but he couldn't stop his thoughts returning to Jim, who'd still be trooping along without a cent to his name. 'How did you lose your property?'

Grantham sighed. 'I was working for this mercantile and I hired a man to make a supply delivery to

19

the Pegasus Lumber Company. The first supply run was fine, but the second never arrived and with Winslow Scott being such a good customer, someone had to take the blame.'

'What are you going to do about it?'

'Drink with you until Pierre's left town.'

Nicholson slapped him on the back. Then they sat quietly, letting Nicholson relax for what felt like the first time since he'd joined Pierre.

He only sipped his drink while Grantham replenished his own glass several times. As Grantham looked at the jail through the window as often as he did, Nicholson asked the obvious question.

'As you no longer have a job and it won't be healthy to remain in town when Murdock Lark gets out of jail, what are you going to do after you've emptied that bottle?'

Grantham considered the nearly empty bottle and then pushed it away.

'What about fighting back, starting with this Pierre Dulaine?'

Nicholson knocked back his drink and winked.

'I thought you'd never ask.'

The two men headed outside. Half of his allotted hour in town had passed, so Nicholson expected that only one man would be guarding the wagon.

As it turned out, Pierre's entire gang had already gathered. Only Pierre wasn't standing with the group; instead he was arguing with Elmina outside the saloon.

Pierre had his hands on his hips and as she was

gesturing angrily at an upstairs bedroom window, Nicholson reckoned her response to Pierre's unsubtle suggestions had turned out to be the one he'd expected.

Their animated argument meant that Pierre's men were ignoring the wagon and so, with the efficiency of men who had once worked together, Nicholson and Grantham got to work.

While Grantham mingled in with the group and asked everyone what the argument was about, Nicholson climbed on to the driver's seat. As his presence wasn't particularly unexpected, despite his having stormed off earlier, Pierre's men ignored him and instead watched the altercation develop.

Elmina berated Pierre while Pierre maintained a contented smile. Nicholson knew Pierre was waiting for her to stop talking so that he could tell her he liked a woman with spirit.

Accordingly, when she stopped shouting and defied him to retort by bending forward, he raised his hat and started to offer the expected retort. He didn't complete it as he found it hard to speak while fending off the carpetbag Elmina slapped against his shoulders.

Her action made the watching men wince and laugh, although their laughter died out when she rained down more blows on their boss. Two men moved forward to help him while Grantham laughed with the other two men.

So, with a casual flick of the reins, Nicholson moved the horses on. The wagon faced into the heart

21

of town and so he directed the horses to circle across the main drag.

This movement didn't elicit a response, as Pierre's men were either trying to drag Elmina away or they were chortling at the sight of the other men trying to drag Elmina away. Grantham took this as his opportunity to back away and, when nobody reacted, he broke into a run.

He caught up with the wagon as Nicholson completed a half-circle. Then, with the open plains beyond the edge of town ahead, he shook the reins.

Only then did consternation break out behind them as Pierre shouted at him to stop.

'Your old boss doesn't sound happy,' Grantham said.

'Hopefully he won't enjoy being taught a lesson about justice.' Nicholson considered. 'And hopefully when we find Jim Dragon he'll know where we can hole up.'

'Agreed, but we have to get out of town first.'

Grantham looked to the edge of town with a pensive expression. Nicholson followed his gaze and he couldn't help but frown, too.

To leave town they'd have to pass the law office and Marshal Collier was standing outside.

The lawman paced forward and raised an imperious hand. In the other hand, he held a six-shooter aimed high.

Nicholson looked for an alternate course of action, but could only see Pierre, who was leading his men in pursuit.

With a sigh, Nicholson drew back on the reins, slowing the wagon. When it had slowed to a walking pace, a heavy thud sounded on the back.

Nicholson glanced over his shoulder as one of Pierre's men, Richard Clancy, vaulted up on to the wagon. He then cringed away as Richard leapt forward, catching him around the shoulders and toppling him from the seat.

He landed on his side on the ground where he curled up to avoid the wheels. His opponent wasn't so cautious and he rolled on top of him and pinned him down.

Above him the wagon rolled forward and it shook as more of Pierre's men leapt on board. Nicholson waited until the back wheels had rolled past before he tried to buck Richard.

He couldn't move him, as Richard had settled his weight down on him. So Nicholson flexed his back against the ground and drove his hips upwards.

When that rolled Richard aside, he leapt to his feet to find Pierre standing before him.

'You'll regret crossing me,' Pierre said, shaking a warning finger.

'My only regret is working for you,' Nicholson said.

Nicholson moved to advance on Pierre, but Richard grabbed his leg and tried to drag him down. Nicholson stumbled forward, but he kept his balance and, anchored to the ground, he launched a scything blow at Pierre's face.

The force of the blow tore Nicholson away from

23

Richard's grasp while his fist connected with Pierre's cheek with a satisfying crunch. Pierre went down on his back and so Nicholson stood over him waiting for him to get up so he could knock him down again.

Pierre was still fingering his face when a shadow passed over his form.

Nicholson looked up to see Marshal Collier had arrived. Behind him Pierre's men had reclaimed the wagon while Grantham was being escorted towards them.

'So Nicholson Perry and Grantham Fletcher are back together again,' Collier said. He set his hands on his hips. 'And I'm not pleased to see that my former deputies have gone bad.'

CHAPTER 3

With a long sigh of relief Jim Dragon cooled the back of his neck using a handful of water from a horse trough.

The walk to town had taken longer than he'd expected and, with sundown close, he didn't reckon Pierre Dulaine would still be here. But when he'd gathered his breath and enjoyed resting in the shadows for a while he still decided to search for him.

He found neither him nor his stolen wagon.

On the other hand, he didn't find anyone who could confirm Pierre had left town either, and so he sat on the edge of the boardwalk outside a bank to take stock of his situation. It didn't take him long.

He was wearing everything he owned and his only asset was the one Pierre couldn't steal. As he needed funds to pursue Pierre, he set about using that asset.

Starting at the jail end of town, he toured the saloons, listening out for anyone talking about work that was suited to his skills.

As he had no money, he couldn't stay in any one

25

place for long and he heard nothing of interest, but an hour after sundown a more worrying feature snagged his attention: two men were following him.

Dragon assumed that his pursuers were being paid by Pierre. The fact that the latter had taken precautions gave him hope that he might find out his rival hadn't gone too far. He decided not to shake off his tails. Instead, he invited trouble by heading to the quieter end of town and walking in the shadows.

He was approaching a well-lit hotel, its windows throwing out long rectangles of light onto the hardpan, when rapid footfalls sounded behind him as his pursuers made their move.

Jim turned as the first man ran into him. In short order he was bundled into the doorway of a mercantile where he was pressed up against the door. A firm punch thudded into his stomach.

The second man kept watch as the first man rocked back to give himself more room, but that gave Jim leeway to act, too. He cringed back against the door while the man swung back his fist, but the moment his assailant launched a second punch at him, he stepped lightly to the side.

The man's fist caught him only a glancing blow before it thudded into the door, making him screech and hunch over his injured hand. Before he could recover, Jim slammed two bunched hands down on the back of his neck, knocking him to his knees and then kicked out, tipping his attacker over and out of the doorway.

When the second man moved in, Jim slipped back

into the shadows.

Having seen the fate of Jim's first assailant, this man was more cautious. He used short paces with his arms spread so he could grab Jim whether he moved to the left or the right, so Jim did neither and ran straight at him.

With a shoulder thrust down he hit the man in the chest and carried him on into the main drag. Jim's speed made both men stumble and they crashed to the ground.

Thankfully, the man fell beneath him and he grunted in pain as Jim's weight landed on him.

Jim added to the man's discomfort by digging in his elbows and fists as he levered himself off him. When he'd clambered to his feet, the other man had gathered his wits and he charged him, using Jim's technique of running shoulder first.

Jim dropped to his knees and hunched his shoulders as he prepared to let the man run into him. His assailant dug in a heel and tried to stop himself, but he failed and so he skidded and folded over Jim's back.

The man somersaulted before landing flat on his back beside his colleague. With a groggy look in his eyes, the man raised himself to feel his back while his colleague fingered his ribs.

Expecting they'd now co-ordinate their next assault, Jim took a slow pace backwards while raising his fists.

Sure enough, the men got to their feet together. They considered him and looked around, presumably to check that nobody had come close while they'd been tussling.

Then, to Jim's surprise, they turned on their heels and ran. They sprinted away from the hotel and, when they'd disappeared into the heart of town, Jim held his fists up to the light to admire them.

'I must look particularly tough tonight,' he said to himself.

'I see losing everything hasn't lowered your high opinion of yourself,' a woman said.

Jim turned to find Elmina Fay was walking towards him from the hotel. She no longer had her bag, but she had drawn her pistol.

'And I see you've decided to repay me for saving you.' Jim gave a short bow. 'I'm much obliged.'

'You should be.' She slipped the gun into a purse. 'Not only did I save your hide, but I showed you the right way to do it.'

'I'll bear that in mind the next time I come across a woman who is apparently in need of help.' He glanced past her at the hotel. 'I assume you had no problem fending off Pierre's advances?'

'I didn't, but it sounds as if you know him well.' She gestured at the hotel. 'I have a room here and I was about to eat. You can join me in the dining room, if you like, and tell me how you know him.'

Jim nodded and beckoned Elmina to lead on. They didn't speak again until they were sitting in the hotel dining room and two plates of steak and potatoes were steaming up the space between them.

'The only thing you need concern yourself with tonight,' Jim said, carving a slice from his steak, 'is that I'm nothing like Pierre Dulaine.'

'That's yet to be proven.' She forked a potato. 'But I now know what his skills are and I have no interest in what he has to offer, but maybe you're different.'

She chewed thoughtfully with her eyebrows raised.

'My skills are all I have now.' He chewed his meat quickly and adopted a serious tone. 'What do you have in mind?'

She worried a second potato while gnawing at her bottom lip.

'Ever since you told me that you're a bone hunter, I've been thinking. Recently, I heard a story about some bones being found like the ones you dig up. I'd like to search for more of them, but I don't know how to start looking and I don't know what I need for such an expedition. You do.'

Jim nodded encouragingly and popped in a second slice of steak.

'Many of my expeditions start with overheard stories, hints and rumours,' he said while chewing. 'What's this story about?'

'It's about Pegasus.'

' "Pegasus"?' Jim spluttered.

'That's what I said.' She narrowed her eyes. 'You do know what Pegasus is, don't you?'

'I do,' Jim said with more conviction than his scant knowledge justified. A laugh tickled his throat and so he gulped down his half-chewed meat. 'It's a mythical beast.'

'A flying horse, to be precise.' She raised an eyebrow inviting a response, but as Jim was struggling

29

to find an appropriately withering comment, she continued. 'You've heard of the Pegasus Lumber Company?'

'I have,' Jim said through gritted teeth to stop himself from laughing until he'd heard the rest of the story.

'It was so named because of a popular local tale about someone digging up a horse with wings.'

Jim pursed his lips, but that failed to keep the laughter in and it emerged in a barking burst of noise that sprayed scraps of meat on to the table and made the other diners glare at him.

'That's a pity,' he said, gasping for air. 'Because I can't dig that flying horse up for a second time.'

She pointed her fork at him. 'You're making fun of me.'

'How did you guess?' Jim raised a hand when her face reddened. 'I like your story, but that's all it is. Pegasus was a mythical creature and the main point about mythical creatures is: they're mythical!'

'I've never seen a giant lizard, but you had the bones of one of them in a crate.'

Jim couldn't argue with that logic and he lowered his head as he sought a way to refuse. He cast his eyes down at his steaming meal.

When his stomach rumbled encouraging him to stop talking and start eating, he looked up.

'I could pretend I believe your story to get a few meals and a few dollars out of you, but that'll just waste your time and mine. I'd sooner earn enough money to track down Pierre.' He waved a hand vaguely. 'And you should go back to doing whatever it was you were doing when I first met you.'

'I understand.' She stabbed her knife into her meat and carved off a slice with a single slash. 'Promise me you'll do whatever you can to help me find the bones of this flying horse and I'll tell you where Pierre's gone.'

'I know where Pierre's gone. He'll be on his way to Bear Creek by now, as I'd planned to do, to sell my bones.'

'You're wrong.' She raised an eyebrow. 'I was with him when he changed his plans.'

With a smile, she popped a thick slice of steak into her mouth. While she chewed slowly, Jim carved another slice of meat, but he sighed and didn't raise it to his mouth.

'All right,' he said with a resigned tone. 'Tell me where Pierre's gone before he gets too far away and I'll help you find your flying horse.'

She jutted her chin and chewed for longer than Jim thought necessary, making a point of showing who was now in control. Then she beckoned him to lean over the table, which he did with a quizzical expression. She leaned forward to whisper in his ear.

'Marshal Collier arrested him. Pierre's sitting in the law office.'

Jim jerked back in his chair. 'If I wasn't eating with you, I could have found that out by myself.'

'You could have.' She chuckled.

Jim stabbed his next slice of meat. 'I'm getting the feeling the two of us will make a good team.'

31

*

'I've not arrested you, yet,' Marshal Collier said. 'So choose your next words carefully.'

'I can only ask that you trust us, like you did when we worked for you,' Nicholson Perry said. He pointed across the law office at Pierre Dulaine. 'That man stole the wagon first.'

'I treat all men the same, so the good work you did for me in the past is irrelevant. Either way, I'm having a hard time believing you stole the wagon back, meaning to return it to the man who had first lost it.'

Nicholson sighed, accepting their story sounded less plausible the more times they repeated it.

For the last few hours they had been held in the law office while the marshal checked out their version of events. When Collier had returned, his sceptical expression suggested Jim Dragon hadn't arrived in town yet and he hadn't been able to find Elmina Fay either.

Despite Jim being the only man who could corroborate their story, Pierre had remained calm, even though the marshal had questioned him as harshly as he'd questioned them.

'Find Jim,' Nicholson said loudly so that Pierre heard him. 'Then the truth will become clear.'

'I hope you're right,' Collier said. 'As then I might have enough time to deal with real problems such as the Pegasus Lumber Company's missing supplies.'

Collier favoured Grantham with a long glare.

'I'm not to blame for that,' Grantham said.

'I never said you were, but I can't help but wonder why you and Nicholson are causing problems on this day of all days.'

'What's so special about today?' Grantham said.

Collier pointed a warning finger at both men in turn.

'Don't play games with me.' He waited for a response that neither man could give and then continued. 'Are you claiming that it's a coincidence you've just met up?'

'I was working for a mercantile and Nicholson was working for Pierre,' Grantham said. 'We both lost our jobs today.'

Collier considered this information and then mustered a begrudging nod.

'In that case, you'll be surprised to hear that Murdock Lark is being released from Beaver Ridge jail at sundown tomorrow.'

Collier wasn't wrong as both men stared at him with open mouths until Nicholson found his voice.

'But Murdock's not due to come out for another nine months.'

'He wasn't, but Winslow Scott has withdrawn all charges.' Collier raised his voice when both men spoke over each other to register their disbelief. 'I don't know why either, but the fact is, tomorrow Murdock will be a free man and you two just happen to be here to greet him.'

'The only thing we'll do if we meet him again is. . . .' Nicholson trailed off when he recalled whom he was speaking to.

'I know how you feel, but you'll stay away from Murdock. If you don't, I'll arrest you no matter what I decide about the ownership of the wagon and those bones.'

Wisely neither man argued, but thankfully they didn't need to when the door opened and two welcome newcomers walked in.

'If you don't want to accept our word,' Nicholson said with a relieved smile as he pointed at them, 'talk to Jim Dragon.'

CHAPTER 4

'That's an interesting story,' Marshal Collier said when Jim Dragon had finished his tale. His irritated tone suggested he thought the opposite.

Jim waved a contemptuous hand at Pierre.

'What he told you is a story,' he said. 'I told you the truth.'

Collier turned to Pierre and, with his shoulders hunched, he tipped back his hat and uttered a weary sigh.

'I assume that'll be your response, too.'

'No,' Pierre said. He put a hand to his chest with a show of wounded pride. 'I would never presume to deal with a lawman in the same arrogant way that Monsieur Dragon does. I have nothing to offer you but my integrity and my dignity.'

Collier blinked hard while Jim tried not to catch anyone's eye.

'So that means,' Collier said after a suitable period of reflective silence, 'I have to choose which one of you is telling the truth about the ownership of a heap of old lizard bones.'

He looked around the crowded law office, taking in each person until his gaze settled on Pierre.

'I'll bow to your superior judgement,' Pierre declared.

'I'm pleased, because I didn't believe a single word you told me.'

Pierre spluttered before he found his voice.

'That's an outrageous slur.'

'On the other hand, I don't believe Jim's story either, and the only men who can back up his account are Nicholson and Grantham, two men I no longer trust.'

'What about me?' Elmina said.

Collier waved a dismissive hand at her. 'I gather you were fighting with Pierre and it took two men to drag you off him. That doesn't make you a reliable witness either.'

As Elmina bowed her head and Jim shook his head sadly, Pierre recovered his composure with a flick of his moustache.

'So what happens to my bones?' he asked.

'I'll keep them until I'm presented with conclusive proof of ownership.' Collier straightened up and pointed at the door. 'And while I wait for that, you'll all leave my office so I can get some real work done!'

Pierre glared at Jim across the office and, despite the setback, Jim returned a smile, reckoning that a chance of getting his property back was better than his previous hopeless position.

Long moments passed in tense silence until, with

neither man showing an inclination to leave, Collier gasped out a long groan of exasperation, but before he could shout at them again, Jim spoke up.

'I assume this real work is the matter everyone's talking about,' he said. 'The Pegasus Lumber Company's missing supplies?'

'It is,' Collier said. 'So unless you know something about their whereabouts, get out.'

'I don't know anything,' Jim spread his arms, inviting Collier to look him up and down. 'But I'm a man who finds things nobody else can and I'd already planned to head north. If I unearth anything that might help you, I'll let you know.'

'Obliged,' Collier said cautiously.

'Don't be,' Pierre said, raising his voice. 'Jim is only trying to get you on his side so you'll believe his lies.'

'I know,' Collier said with a smile. 'And he's going about it in the right way.'

Pierre snorted with disdain. 'I would never stoop to such low-down tactics.'

Collier sighed. 'I know that, too. You have only your integrity and your dignity to offer me.'

'And a complete lack of ability to find anything,' Jim said as Pierre bristled.

As he reckoned his last unsubtle comment might have overstated his case, Jim headed for the door. Elmina hurried on to join him closely followed by Nicholson and Grantham.

Once outside, Jim kept walking, not wanting to be waylaid by Pierre while he had his hired men with him.

'I hope you'll still fulfil your earlier promise to me,' Elmina said when Jim could see the hotel ahead.

'Of course,' Jim said. 'Now that my bones are safe with the lawman, I've been gifted a way to convince him that I told the truth about my abilities while showing you I can fulfil your dreams.'

'Pierre promised to do that, too.' She leaned towards him and smiled. 'I kicked him so hard I doubt he'll fulfil any woman's dreams for a while.'

She walked on ahead and Jim stopped to wince. Then he checked over his shoulder. Pierre hadn't followed him and for that matter neither had Nicholson and Grantham.

He smiled and hurried on after Elmina.

'I thought you said liquor didn't solve nothing,' Grantham said.

'It doesn't,' Nicholson said, knocking back his drink, 'but if I drink enough tonight, it might get me in the right mood to solve everything tomorrow.'

When Nicholson turned to the door, Grantham brightened for the first time since they'd left the law office. Then he pushed his empty glass away.

The saloon they were in wasn't the one they'd been in before and the jail wasn't visible, so the two men headed outside.

'Three months in there must have been tough for Murdock Lark,' Grantham said after contemplating the foreboding building. 'He'll be tired, weak.'

'But not for long. If we're going to do anything, we

have to make our move before he gets his wits about him.'

Grantham slapped his shoulder. 'Talk like that is good to hear, but I can't see it working. All we'll achieve from going after Murdock is making sure he comes after us.'

Nicholson gave a reluctant nod. Then the two men strolled down the main drag with their gazes set on the jail.

'So that means we have to leave town tomorrow and slink off with our tails between our legs,' Nicholson said when they were approaching the hotel where Jim Dragon had taken a room for the night.

Grantham started to agree, but then Pierre Dulaine stepped out from the shadows beside a mercantile.

'I was keeping an eye on Monsieur Dragon,' Pierre said happily. 'I see you've had the same idea, although I presume our intentions differ.'

With the route ahead blocked, Nicholson glanced over his shoulder and he wasn't surprised that two of Pierre's men were standing at the other corner of the building.

'Jim won't be pleased with me either,' he said, matching Pierre's relaxed tone and demeanour. 'If I hadn't got involved, Marshal Collier might have accepted his word that he owned the bones.'

Pierre dismissed his attempt to lessen the extent of his duplicity with a waft of the hand.

'But if you hadn't got involved, Collier would

never have been concerned with that question in the first place.'

Nicholson conceded the point with a nod. Then, with a glance at Grantham, he spun round and set off at a run.

Richard Clancy moved to block his path. At the last moment Nicholson tried to swerve aside, but as he jammed a foot down he noticed something on the ground.

He'd just worked out that he'd stepped into a noose when the rope tightened around his ankle. Then he was upended and, with a thud, he landed on his chest.

As he was hauled in, through his stunned senses he noted that Pierre's other two men were lurking in the shadows beside the mercantile.

By then it was too late to do anything about it. He was surrounded.

He was dragged to his feet and Pierre's men jostled for position. They all got in kicks and punches as the rope was wrapped around him.

By the time he'd been bound securely, two men had pinned Grantham to the ground. Then Nicholson was bundled away to stand before Pierre, who leaned back against the wall with a foot raised nonchalantly on a discarded crate.

'If you harm us, Marshal Collier will come after you,' Nicholson said.

'That's the worst threat I've ever heard,' Pierre said. 'I have a better one. Your attempt to steal my wagon made me lose my bones. You'll get them back.'

'The only way I can do that is to convince the marshal you're not a conniving, double-crossing snake with the morals of a moth-eaten cat and the charm of a dead skunk.'

His captors tensed, but Pierre shrugged without concern.

'Your task is hard, but the reward will make it worthwhile.' Pierre nodded to Richard who tensed and drew Nicholson closer. 'My bones are worth thousands of dollars and without them I can't pay your former associates. This news has not made them sociable.'

Richard drew the rope tightly around his waist and muttered an oath in his ear.

'Collier offered you a way out,' Nicholson said, jerking his head away from Richard's hot breath. 'He's sure to believe whoever finds the missing supplies.'

'Such tasks are suited to men like Monsieur Dragon who enjoy rooting around in the dirt like a bug.' Pierre batted dust from his sleeve with apparent distaste. 'I prefer to let others soil their hands.'

'If you can't find them, I surely won't.'

Pierre sighed. 'You've clearly not yet appreciated the pain I can make you suffer.'

Pierre gave a casual wave and Richard thudded a pile-driver of a punch into Nicholson's side. Constrained by the ropes Nicholson could only stand rigidly and take his punishment.

Two men stood on either side of him and drove punches into his ribs until a backhanded swipe to the cheek made him thud into the wall face first. His bound legs ensured he couldn't move and he stood with his cheek pressed against the wall before he slid down it to land on his knees on the ground.

While he struggled to stand up, Grantham's two assailants knocked Grantham back and forth until Nicholson was dragged back to his feet.

A gut-wrenching punch to the belly made Nicholson fold over coughing bile. Blows thudded into his ribs making him straighten. Then another backhanded swipe sent him spinning into the wall.

Again, he slid down it only to be dragged back to his feet. Then the operation began all over again.

His only consolation was the thought that at least Pierre didn't want him dead, for now.

His world contracted to a whirling vision of fists, boots, and the ground appearing to come up to meet him. The only constant was the pain and the fact that his demands for the torment to end went unanswered.

So it came as a surprise when he tensed for a blow and it didn't come.

He opened his eyes to find he was lying on the ground while Grantham lay on his back a few feet away. With his legs still being constrained, Nicholson wriggled towards him, but that movement made his ribs protest and so he pressed his forehead to the dirt.

He breathed shallowly until Pierre grabbed a handful of hair and dragged his head up. With mock concern curling his upper lip Pierre considered him.

'Have you appreciated yet how much I want my bones back?' he said.

'Sure,' Nicholson murmured through bleeding lips.

Pierre opened his hand letting Nicholson's head slam back down into the dirt. Then he wiped his hand on Nicholson's sleeve.

'Good. I don't care how you get them. Find the supplies, steal the bones, kill Monsieur Dragon . . . it doesn't matter at all to me. All that matters is that you do it, or the only way you'll leave Beaver Ridge is in a coffin.'

CHAPTER 5

Ten miles out of Beaver Ridge, Jim Dragon started whistling as the thrill of starting a new quest restored his usual good spirits – even if his quest was a futile one and consisted of finding a creature that had never existed.

The futility didn't appear to concern Elmina and she had been as good as her word. She had accepted his list of requirements without question and then had accompanied him around town to purchase a wagon, replacement tools and provisions.

After each bargain had been concluded, and Jim prided himself on ensuring the seller's scowl at the end of the negotiation was real, she had fished into her bag and produced the necessary cash. He hadn't asked her about how much money was in the bag, but her lack of concern about the mounting expenditure suggested their purchases hadn't dented her finances.

In fact, his whistling was the first thing that day

that had appeared to concern her as, the moment he began, she turned in the seat to glare at him.

'Be quiet, or this will be a very long journey,' she said.

'It is a long journey, but we should still reach our first destination of Martin's Pass before sundown.'

'We're not going to Martin's Pass.'

She jutted her chin, confirming his observation last night that she would try to control him by being frugal with the information she revealed. In other circumstances this would have annoyed him, but as his mission was to help her achieve the impossible, he could only smile.

He filled the quiet period by putting his mind to how he could accomplish the more achievable quest of locating the missing supplies.

Last night, he had asked around town, but he had learnt little other than the basic facts that a supply wagon had left Beaver Ridge a week ago.

The wagon had trundled through Martin's Pass on schedule, but it hadn't reached its final destination another day away at the Pegasus Lumber Company located up in the hills. As these scant details didn't provide enough information to give him an edge over the company men who were already searching for it, he spoke up.

'We can't avoid the only settlement out here,' he said.

She shrugged. 'We've bought enough provisions for a long expedition.'

'I'd prefer a short, successful expedition and we

won't be successful if we don't get more information.'

She pursed her lips. 'Would that be successful in finding my flying horse or in finding the missing supplies?'

Jim granted her a smile. 'I hope to do both and we need a place to start with both of the searches.'

'I already have all the information you'll need to look for the flying horse.' She started to jut her jaw, but when that made him smile, she continued. 'We'll start at a place a day's ride beyond Martin's Pass.'

They rode on in silence for a while.

'If it helps, as I told you before, I'm not like Pierre Dulaine,' Jim said in a low tone. 'I keep my promises. Last night, I promised to help you find the bones of a flying horse and I'll do everything I can to make sure you complete your quest.'

She nodded, seemingly content with his choice of words that had carefully avoided promising her the impossible while leaving him free to do the minimum a hopeless quest deserved.

'We'll visit a trading post beside the new railroad tracks. There'll be a depot there soon and before long it's sure to attract more people.' She turned to him and grinned. 'The place is called Pegasus Heights.'

Jim sighed. 'Of course it is.'

'The owner Archibald Brown can tell you about the local legend, and I guess he'll also help you narrow down your other search depending on whether or not he saw the supplies go by.'

'I'm sure he will,' Jim said brightening. 'And it sounds as if you already know a lot about this place. Was Pegasus Heights where you were coming from when I first met you walking along the trail?'

She jutted her jaw, this time with a more determined gesture than before.

'What I was doing is none of your business,' she declared.

'Nobody knows nothing about the missing supplies,' Grantham Fletcher said when he came out of the last saloon on the main drag.

Nicholson Perry had already reached that conclusion three saloons ago and so while Grantham had been asking inside, he had sat slumped on the edge of the boardwalk.

The low sun was casting sallow light across the jail's walls and barred windows. While he rubbed his bruised ribs, he decided that Murdock Lark wouldn't expect that he and Grantham would be in town.

With that promising thought cheering him, he raised himself. But, after his beating, he struggled to gain his feet and Grantham had to help him up.

'On the other hand I don't reckon anyone was hiding anything,' Nicholson said as they moved on.

Grantham nodded. 'I wouldn't have believed anyone if they had claimed they knew who stole the supplies, except nobody did.'

Nicholson stopped to stretch, freeing the tightness from his chest.

'If we can't find anyone who knows what's happened, we'll have to leave town and search for the supplies ourselves.'

'Leaving would be the better option rather than spending the next few days waiting until Murdock comes across us.'

They walked on until they reached the last building on the edge of town and only the jail was ahead. The sun was an outstretched hand's width from the horizon.

Activity was going on around the gate making them wince, but before they could move away, Nicholson discerned what was happening.

A wagon driven by Marshal Collier had stopped. He spoke to the guards at the gate and then moved on without picking anyone up.

They waited and, when the marshal drew up the wagon beside them, he considered their battered clothes and their even more battered visages.

'You two want to report anything?' he asked.

'We fell over,' Nicholson said.

'Several times,' Grantham added.

Collier shook his head and glanced at the horizon where the sun was disappearing behind a cloud. He jumped down from the wagon to join them in facing the jail.

He said nothing and, after the silence had dragged on until the sun emerged from under the cloud as a foreshortened red orb, Nicholson accepted he was testing their resolve.

'We don't want to be standing here come sundown,'

Nicholson said.

'I'm pleased to hear it,' Collier said. 'If I were you, I wouldn't even be in town come sundown.'

'It's too late to do anything about that now, but we're leaving tomorrow.'

'That's good news.' Collier beckoned them to the back of the wagon. 'I followed the trail the supply wagon took and twenty miles out of town I found a body I don't recognize.'

Collier clambered into the back of the wagon to kneel beside a body lying under a blanket.

Grantham climbed up and raised the blanket. His eyebrows shot up before he removed the rest of the blanket to reveal a bullet wound that had reddened the body's chest.

'This is Igor Rodgers,' Grantham said with a wince. 'He's the man I hired to deliver the supplies that have gone missing.'

CHAPTER 6

As Elmina had promised, the Pegasus Heights trading post stood 200 yards from the rail tracks. Dozens of piles of timber were behind the building suggesting that before long, the promised depot would be built.

With the area being flat and with a creek nearby, Jim reckoned Elmina was right and that this place would expand rapidly, but for now the area was deserted and the post was quiet.

Jim let Elmina take the lead in heading inside. He was intrigued to see how Archibald reacted to her as it might help to explain what she'd been doing before he'd met her.

When they'd made camp last night, several miles to the east of Martin's Pass, he'd probed her for information about her life, but she'd expertly ignored his questions.

Instead, he'd talked about his own exploits, which she'd been fascinated to hear about, although later, as he tried to get to sleep, he wondered if she had just let him talk so she didn't have to.

The post was being minded by a surly individual who identified himself as Archibald and he became even surlier when it became clear Elmina wanted information, not supplies. Jim stepped in.

'We're looking for something valuable,' he said, rattling the coins in his pocket.

Archibald leaned on the counter and favoured them with a smile for the first time.

'How valuable?'

Jim smiled. 'Don't you want to know what we're looking for first?'

'I can find out anything, for the right price.'

'Even if I want to know what happened to the missing supplies for the Pegasus Lumber Company?'

A momentary darkness shadowed Archibald's features before he masked his concern by rubbing his face and coming out from behind the counter. He headed to the window to look at the railroad.

'That's a worrying development and if I knew who'd stolen them, I'd tell you for nothing. Winslow Scott has been good to us and life will be even better before long. If he gets concerned about security because of this, the railroad might have second thoughts, too.'

He sighed and turned back to them while shrugging. His manner provoked a sympathetic frown from Elmina, but Jim reckoned Archibald's speech had been too long and it had sounded too sincere to be believed.

'Why did Winslow buy supplies from Beaver Ridge

when he could have got them here?'

Archibald shrugged. 'He can't get everything he needs here.'

'I'd have expected that a man who can get anything for the right price would be able to supply him.'

'I have no problem with Winslow,' Archibald snapped, his anger confirming that Jim might have touched a raw nerve.

'So did the supply wagon pass by?' Jim asked, softening his tone so as not to provoke Archibald further.

'It did, but I gather it never reached its destination.' Archibald pointed north.

Jim joined him at the window and looked along the route he'd indicated, not because he intended to follow the exact route, but because he couldn't bring himself to ask the next question.

To his relief, Elmina spoke up.

'Thankfully we're concerned about more than just the missing supplies,' she said. 'We were also interesting in hearing about Pegasus.'

Jim braced himself for ridicule, but Archibald nodded in a casual manner, as if he'd often been asked this question. He headed back behind the counter and gave them both a wide smile.

'For a dollar I'll tell you the story I tell everyone. For five dollars I'll tell you the full story. For ten dollars I'll take you there.'

Elmina dropped her bag to the floor and opened it up.

Jim knew how much money she'd take out and so he stood between her and the counter. Then, when she withdrew the money, he split it in half and handed five dollars back to her, a wink being his only explanation.

'Two dollars buys us the truth,' he said, turning to Archibald. 'Three dollars will be your reward if we like it.'

Archibald nodded while licking his lips, his eyes bright as he prepared to launch into his tale. The moment Jim slapped the money down on the counter, he started up while waving his arms with animated delight.

'Ten years ago,' he said with a lively tone that made Jim groan and Elmina nod, possibly confirming she'd heard these words before, 'on a warm and sleepy day, something strange happened not far from this very spot. That event was to change forever the lives of everyone who witnessed the magical—'

Jim threw the remaining three dollars on the table.

'I'll give you the three dollars now if you skip to the ending,' he said.

Archibald narrowed his eyes, but thankfully he lowered his arms.

'A successful gold prospector bound for Beaver Ridge bought supplies here,' he said using a clipped tone. 'He went missing. I searched. I found his wagon perched on the top of an outcrop. He was dead. His gold was gone. I called the outcrop Pegasus Heights.'

Archibald clamped a hand over the three dollars with a triumphant gleam in his eye that defied Jim to complain after he had demanded the short version of the story.

'Is that because you found the bones of a . . .' Jim trailed off and took a deep breath. 'Did you find the skeleton of a flying horse on the top of Pegasus Heights?'

'No,' Archibald said with a furrowed brow that made Elmina laugh. 'Who gave you that idea?'

'Elmina was convinced someone had found bones.' He looked at Archibald and then at Elmina, and they were both smiling. He set his hands on his hips. 'What have I missed here?'

'I didn't find the bones of a dead flying horse,' Archibald said while waggling his hands at shoulder height in a depiction of flapping wings. 'No, I found a live flying horse!'

Jim groaned and banged his forehead on the counter three times. Then he groaned some more.

The stables appeared to be deserted.

For the last hour Nicholson and Grantham had watched the building from the shadows at the side of a hotel. Through the open doorway they could see the two horses they'd bought this morning with the last of their funds.

They had hoped to leave town after completing the transaction, but then Pierre had strolled by the stable and so they'd postponed their flight.

'Come on,' Nicholson said, slapping Grantham's

shoulder. 'Nobody's gone in or out of the stable for thirty minutes.'

Grantham glanced around the corner of the hotel and then nodded.

'And there's plenty of people about,' he said. 'We should be able to mingle in.'

With that decided, they set off across the main drag. They chatted animatedly, ensuring they didn't attract undue attention.

At the stable door, Grantham stopped and batted dust from his boots while leaning against the wall. While Graham kept watch, Nicholson carried on into the stables, but the moment his eyes became accustomed to the gloom inside, he saw two of Pierre's men standing in the shadows.

When they saw him they set off purposefully. Nicholson moved towards the nearest stall, but that made them speed up and so he turned on his heel.

He ran back to the doorway where he skidded to a halt when Grantham hurried into view.

Grantham pointed over his shoulder, his worried expression telling Nicholson everything he needed to know. Then Grantham ran past him, and he didn't slow down when he saw the two men.

As Nicholson turned, Grantham barged the first man aside and launched a scything punch on the run that grounded the second man.

Nicholson ran after him. He punched the first man as that man moved to get to his feet, knocking him back down, and leapt over the second man.

They would still need time to get their horses

ready to leave and so they hunkered down behind the corner post and drew their guns.

A few moments later, Pierre Dulaine moved into the doorway with his other two men flanking him. These men levelled guns on them and so they both aimed at Pierre.

'Stand-off, Pierre,' Nicholson said.

'I have two guns on you,' Pierre said without concern. He gestured at the two prone men to get up, which they did while drawing their guns. 'And now I have four, which means you are going nowhere.'

'The only thing that matters is that we're both aiming guns at you. If we're going nowhere, neither will you.'

Pierre narrowed his eyes, appearing uncertain for the first time.

'I gave you a way out. Yet I still don't have my bones.'

Nicholson stood up, the fact that Pierre was talking giving him hope they might reach an agreement.

'It wasn't an easy task, but we've been working on it.'

'You'd have found it easier if you hadn't been hiding while plotting how you'd sneak out of town without my noticing.'

Nicholson conceded his point with a smile and he lowered his gun slightly before he made his offer.

'We were sneaking out of town, but we still plan to find the missing supplies and so convince Marshal

Collier you're a man to be trusted.'

Pierre raised a hand, making Nicholson tense, but to his surprise his men lowered their guns.

'I agree with your plan. In fact, I like it so much I'll accompany you.' Pierre raised an eyebrow. 'I assume while you were asking around town you gathered useful information and so you have a place to start your search?'

'We do,' Nicholson said, reckoning that was the only answer he should give.

When he and Grantham holstered their guns, Pierre moved to turn away, but then he swung back and offered a sly smile.

'I should mention that I've hired a man who knows the area. He's looking forward to working with you.'

Nicholson was familiar with Pierre's sneaky behaviour and so he gulped.

Sure enough, when the new hired man strode into the stable, there was no mistaking Murdock Lark's massive frame that appeared on its own to reduce the amount of light coming into the stables.

With his customary long stride Murdock stormed across the stables making Nicholson and Grantham shuffle backwards.

'Nicholson Perry and Grantham Fletcher,' Murdock rumbled when he stomped to a halt before them, his grating voice like hammer blows on rocks. 'Two men I never thought I'd see again, alive.'

Murdock flared his eyes and then while taking a step forward he launched a scything backhanded blow to Grantham's chin that cracked his head back and sent him spinning to the ground. He advanced on Nicholson, who just had enough time to raise an arm before his face.

Murdock battered the arm aside. Then he slapped his hand over Nicholson's face and pushed.

Nicholson went staggering backwards until the back of his head smashed into the wall with a sickening thud. Then merciful oblivion seized him.

CHAPTER 7

'You did promise to do everything you could to help me,' Elmina said after they'd ridden along for a few miles.

'And I am,' Jim said, 'I bought us all the information Archibald Brown had on your flying horse. Now, I'm taking you to the outcrop where he claims he saw it.'

Jim hadn't been able to disguise the irritation in his voice and so he wasn't surprised when Elmina muttered to herself.

'I thought you specialized in difficult quests like this one. When I hired you, I didn't think you'd behave in such an uninterested way.'

'Believe me, if I'd done what I'd wanted to do, I'd have left you at the trading post and I'd now be using the scraps of real information I learnt there to find the missing supplies.'

'You can do that when I have Pegasus.'

She stared at him triumphantly, defying him to refuse. Jim couldn't think of a retort and so he concentrated on looking out for the landmarks

Archibald had described.

He'd been promised Pegasus Heights was impossible to miss, although from the direction they approached it, they were a half-mile away when the outcrop poked out from beyond a rise. Jim directed the wagon over a lower point beside the summit of the rise.

When the scene beyond came into view, he stopped the wagon, feeling impressed despite his own misgivings.

A round lake was below. It was a quarter-mile across and it had been formed in the bowl-like depression made by the surrounding hills.

Set in the lake close to their side was an outcrop. It was about a hundred feet high and wide, its presence looking incongruous and its rocky nature unlike the gentle swell of the hills.

'I can see why Archibald views this place with awe,' Jim said.

Elmina acknowledged Jim's first sign of enthusiasm with a smile.

'If ever there was a place where Pegasus lived, this would be it,' she said.

Jim jumped down from the wagon. He walked back and forth considering the lie of the land with a practiced eye until Elmina joined him.

'If you're prepared to accept that I know what I'm talking about, I have to tell you that the kind of terrain where I've found fossils before looks nothing like this place.'

'You heard Archibald's story. We're not looking

for bones any more.'

'No, but perhaps we might find the bottles of rot-gutting whiskey he was drinking on the night he saw a horse come flapping by and then roost up on that outcrop.'

Jim flapped his arms in a parody of Archibald's actions when describing his encounter.

'I agree his story sounded like a drunken vision.' She waited until Jim sighed with relief and then continued. 'But until you can explain why ten years ago he only found the missing prospector's wagon standing on the top of that outcrop and not the flying horse which flew it there, keep those thoughts to yourself.'

Jim rubbed his jaw. 'If I find a reason, will you give up on this quest?'

'If Archibald's story is just a story, I have no reason to be here and you have no reason to delay searching for the supplies.'

Jim accepted her revised challenge with a nod. Then, while fingering his shark's tooth, he did as he'd been asked to do and pondered.

Archibald had clearly told the story many times about his search for the missing prospector and its unlikely conclusion. Like all oft-told tales, over the years it would have become more outlandish and only a grain of truth about the original events would remain.

It followed that the most likely explanations were that Archibald was either lying about the facts, or he had embellished them too much.

Only some of the prospector's possessions could have been left on the top of Pegasus Heights after the prospector had holed up there. Or he could have found the wagon on the shore of the lake all smashed up and looking as if it'd fallen from a great height.

The one element of the story that was clearly false was that when Archibald had climbed to the top of the outcrop, he had found a winged horse. It had been rigged up to the wagon, but now it was free and when he'd spooked it, the horse had flown off never to be seen again.

He doubted he could prove this was a fabrication until he'd heard other people's opinions on Archibald. So he kept his scepticism to himself as he climbed back on the wagon and headed off.

At the water's edge and in the shadow of Pegasus Heights, he moved the wagon on while examining the outcrop.

Archibald had been right that it was so steep only a determined man could climb it and neither a horse nor a wagon should have been able to reach the top even if they could get across the water.

When they emerged from the shadow, he drew the wagon to a halt.

'I don't have an explanation other than that Archibald's story never happened,' he said, turning to Elmina.

'And how have you reached that conclusion?' she said.

'Putting aside the fact that flying horses don't

exist, a wagon couldn't have been standing on the top of an outcrop in the middle of the lake when anyone would struggle to swim the lake, never mind climb Pegasus Heights.'

He set his hands on his hips, putting the onus on her to now provide an explanation rather than just disagreeing with his.

She took her time, looking the outcrop over and nodding. Then she put her hand to her brow and brightened.

'Would that convince you it's possible?' she asked, pointing.

Jim turned in his seat and peered up at the point on Pegasus Heights that she'd indicated. He blinked in surprise and then put a hand to his brow.

Being able to see clearly without the low sun in his eyes didn't change the fact that a wagon was standing on the top of the outcrop in a position that wasn't visible from elsewhere along the water's edge.

'Yeah, that would do it,' he said with a sigh.

CHAPTER 8

When the wagon drew to a halt, hands slapped down on Nicholson's back and pushed him forward.

The motion made him groan as muscles that had been trapped in cramped positions for hours protested.

His hands had been tied behind his back and his legs had been strapped together. A gag remained in his mouth and a sack was still over his head.

He could therefore do nothing to cushion his fall when the tailboard was lowered and he was tipped off the wagon. Thankfully, he landed on soft ground and he rolled, thereby avoiding Grantham when he too was shoved off the wagon.

Their captors gathered a short distance away where they talked in low tones until Pierre Dulaine spoke up.

'These men are responsible for my current difficulties, but they have a plan to get my property back,' he said, 'I can't let you kill them.'

Even if Nicholson hadn't known Pierre, he'd have

noted the staged nature of that declaration. In reply, Murdock Lark rumbled an oath.

As Nicholson had expected, footsteps approached. Then the sack was whipped from his head and his gag was dragged away.

While Grantham received the same treatment, Nicholson glanced around.

It was dark and the only light came from two brands that created a semicircle of light on the ground stretching beyond the wagon. Nicholson worked out the circle wasn't complete because the land fell away beside the wagon.

He heard water running by below confirming they were on the edge of a long drop; his observations served to clarify their fate should they fail to please Pierre.

So when Nicholson faced his former boss, he spoke using a neutral tone that neither begged nor defied him, figuring only the truth would save them.

'You first hired me because I was experienced at hunting men,' he said. 'Sure enough, I helped you find Jim Dragon. Now, I intend to find the missing supplies.'

'How?'

'We picked up no clues in town.' Nicholson shrugged when that declaration made Pierre sneer. 'I'd have expected someone to know something, or for there to be rumours, but we heard nothing, and that's interesting.'

Pierre nodded, his expression softening for the first time.

'Anyone who knows anything had their silence bought.'

Nicholson smiled. 'And there's more. Only supplies have gone missing and yet Winslow Scott and the marshal are mighty concerned. That suggests there's more going on here than anyone's admitting.'

Pierre raised an eyebrow in approval and then walked back and forth past his and Grantham's supine forms before he faced Murdock.

'Nicholson has spoken a lot of sense,' he said. 'Can you better that?'

'If you don't give them to me, I'll tear your head off,' Murdock said.

Pierre smiled and walked back and forth again, the movement masking a glance he gave to his men. They tensed while Murdock merely folded his arms and set his feet wider apart.

Pierre stopped walking. 'You've eloquently argued your case, too, but perhaps we can still reach an agreement.'

'Yeah, you stop talking and I'll give them three months' worth of pain before I toss their bodies in the river.'

Murdock advanced on Pierre and a moment later four guns were aimed at him. Murdock stomped to a halt, but he did so in a deliberate manner that implied he'd chosen to stop rather than that he'd been forced to.

'You can still do that,' Pierre said, spreading his arms as he backed away for a pace. 'But only after they and you have dealt with my problem.'

Murdock took another long pace forward to loom over Nicholson and Grantham. Neither man could meet his gaze and so he snorted with contempt and swung round to face Pierre.

'I accept your deal. We'll ride together, but once this is over, you won't stop me dealing with them.'

'Of course,' Pierre said. 'What happens when this is over is no concern of mine.'

When Murdock folded his arms, Pierre's men moved in to untie Nicholson's bonds. The moment he was free, Nicholson crawled away and Grantham did the same.

Then the two men helped each other to their feet and shuffled towards the wagon, freeing the cramp from their muscles. As Pierre's men started to plan their next move, Murdock moved closer and blocked their path.

'I had three months to plan what I'd do to you when I came out,' he said.

'We defeated you the last time and we can do it again,' Nicholson said with a snarl of defiance.

Murdock shook his head and glanced at the other men, all of whom were watching this confrontation. He licked his lips.

'Have you heard the rumour about what happened to the outlaw we were all looking for, Chadwick Jackson?' He waited until Nicholson nodded. Then he leaned towards them and lowered his voice to a grating whisper. 'It was no rumour. I did it.'

Nicholson gulped and Grantham failed to hide his horror as he put a hand to his mouth, making Murdock laugh. Then he barged his way between them.

Murdock joined Pierre, who backed away with his upper lip curled with concern. When his men turned away to make camp, nobody met Murdock's gaze.

CHAPTER 9

'That'll never float,' Elmina said when Jim proudly stepped back from his creation.

'Wood floats,' Jim said. 'This raft is made of wood, It'll float.'

He set his hands on his hips, defying her to argue with his logic. She considered the raft with disdain and shook her head.

'I'm not going out onto the water on that.'

'Then that's a bonus.'

Jim turned his back on her ensuring he got in the last word. Then he considered how he would use his creation without suffering the indignity of proving she had been right.

Since first light he had worked on his raft. He had dragged four tree trunks that had washed up at the side of the lake out of the water.

Then he'd lashed the trunks together to create a crude, misshapen raft that was five times longer than it was wide, but without tools he didn't think he could have done better.

He judged his biggest problem was steering the raft. As the logs had washed up here, to reach Pegasus Heights he'd have to fight against the prevailing current that moved water towards him.

He headed to the wagon and rummaged until he located a discarded plank of wood that fitted his hand well. When he returned to the lake, to his amusement, Elmina was standing by the raft and looking for the best way to climb on board.

Resting on her shoulder was a paddle she had fashioned from a branch by stripping away the smaller branches to leave a pole with leafy twigs at one end.

Jim made no comment and he stood back while she crawled on to the raft.

On hands and knees, she moved to a point where she was kneeling above the water. Then she shuffled round to sit facing the outcrop with her legs drawn up to her chest and her feet tucked under the rope.

When she waved him on, Jim put his hands to the end of the longest log and shoved.

His first effort failed to move the raft for even an inch. His second try made him slip on the damp ground and his third attempt landed him on his rump.

He jumped back up but, thankfully, Elmina appeared not to have noticed, as she was busy practicing rowing techniques in the shallow water. While rubbing his back he stood back and tried to fight down his growing irritation.

He'd struggled to drag the tree trunks out of the

water and so he should have realized that four logs lashed together would be even harder to move.

Worse, Elmina nodded, appearing to accept she'd found the right way to row, and glanced over her shoulder at him with an eyebrow raised as she silently asked the obvious question.

Unwilling to accept he'd erred, Jim grabbed a spare log and lay it beside the raft. Then he crammed a second log beneath the raft and, using it as a lever, he bore down.

At first, nothing moved and so he raised himself and bent over the log until his toes were suspended a foot off the ground.

With a series of sucking sounds the raft came free of the mud and so he jiggled up and down, increasing the noise.

A crack sounded, and a moment later he was lying on his belly in the mud. This time, he didn't bother trying to maintain his dignity by leaping to his feet and he lay there listening to Elmina laugh with high-pitched peels that sounded farther and farther away.

He got up to see his plan had worked and the raft was sliding into the water. Then he had to run and leap to clamber aboard the logs before they sailed off without him.

His action gave the raft more impetus and while he lay on his side gathering his breath, the raft surged through the water towards the outcrop in a satisfying way that nullified his embarrassment.

When the momentum had died, he joined Elmina in paddling. Before long, his satisfaction had faded, too, as they faced the reality of steering a cumbersome raft that appeared to have made up its own mind about where it wanted to go.

They veered to the right and no matter how fast they paddled, the craft continued to move in that direction until they were facing back towards the side of the lake.

Although Jim judged they'd moved away from the land, he still slapped the water in frustration when the raft continued its steady circling motion and took the land out of view.

'Stop splashing,' Elmina shouted. 'Leave me to paddle.'

'Without my help you'll never get this big raft to Pegasus Heights,' Jim said.

'I'm always better off without your help, so stop fighting against me!'

She glared at him over her shoulder and, as the raft was now swinging back to point at the outcrop again, he stopped swirling his paddle and raised it from the water with a resigned gesture.

She said nothing more and turned to the front where she began paddling, alternating between stroking on one side and then the other. This action stopped the raft from swirling around in the water, but Jim also judged they were only inching forward.

Acting quietly so she wouldn't notice, he experimented with paddling gently until he found a rhythm that worked with her by rowing in time with her movements.

He concentrated on his own movements and so,

when he next took note of their progress, they'd moved for half of the way to the outcrop. They were even approaching the section he'd wanted to reach where there was a stretch of low rocks.

Elmina slowed her paddling as she considered the area where they'd fetch up. So Jim stopped paddling and let her direct the raft, which she did with surprising grace.

The raft turned slowly until they were side-on to Pegasus Heights. Then they drifted in until they bumped up against a rock.

Jim hadn't considered how they'd then disembark, but she appeared to have worked out the required actions already. She unfurled the dangling end of the rope with which she'd kept her feet in position and swung it over a boulder.

It took her three attempts before the rope caught, after which she secured the raft. Only then did she turn around, and Jim had no difficulty in directing an admiring tip of the hat to her.

'It seems you are better off without my help,' he said.

She snorted, as if this was obvious, and peered up the outcrop.

'Doing nothing is the most sensible thing you've done so far,' she declared.

Jim rolled forward on to his knees and crawled along the length of the raft. As she looked uncertain about her next movement, he clambered onto the rocks first and, standing on the boulder, he held out a hand.

'My raft didn't sink though,' he said as he drew her up to join him.

'Yet,' she said, and moved off to the slope.

Jim let her take the lead. He figured that if she were to slip, he was in a good position to still her fall, but she moved on with determined steps using her hands to draw herself up over the steepest sections.

Within a minute she'd clambered on until she was well ahead of him and after another minute he'd lost sight of her.

The climb was around a hundred feet with the rocks being slippery and so he didn't try to catch up with her. When he emerged on to the top of the outcrop, she was standing before the abandoned wagon with her hands on her hips.

From the side of the lake, Jim had been unable to tell if this wagon was the one Archibald Brown had talked about, but from closer to, it was clear that it hadn't stood here for ten years.

Although battered and rickety, the wagon was clean and intact, and painted along both sides was a slogan that proclaimed the wagon was the property of the Pegasus Lumber Company. Above the words was a carving of a rearing winged horse that was secured into the wood with thick tar.

On the back were several crates with their lids lying askew.

Still feeling bemused, Jim clambered on to the back and pushed the lids further aside to reveal there was nothing inside any of them other than a few rocks.

74

He shook away the thought that in the past he had often fooled Pierre Dulaine by leading him to crates like these that had rocks in them instead of bones.

He figured this was probably the wagon that had carried the missing supplies. Somehow, it had been left abandoned in a place where no wagon should ever be.

He considered the picture of a flying horse on the lid and dismissed that explanation of how it had got here with a laugh.

Then he turned to Elmina, who was considering the wagon with a watery-eyed expression; as this was so different from her usual feisty attitude, it took him a few moments to understand it.

When he decided that she looked disappointed, he jumped down and stood before her.

'Our quest ends now,' he said, 'unless you tell me who you are, what you really want, what you were doing when I first met you, and what you expected to find here.'

'What happened between you three?' Richard Clancy asked.

This was the first pleasant thing that Richard, or for that matter anyone in the group, had said to Nicholson and Grantham since they'd joined forces to find the supplies.

As he and Richard had often spoken before he'd turned on Pierre, Nicholson welcomed this thawing in the frosty atmosphere.

Since setting off that morning, they had travelled

quickly and they were now close to Martin's Pass. Pierre hadn't wanted to head into town and so they'd rested up in the open.

The men sat along the banks of the river with significant distances between Murdock and Pierre's men and between the men and Nicholson and Grantham.

'It's a long story,' Nicholson said.

'I've heard some of it,' Richard shrugged, 'Or at least I've heard rumours.'

Nicholson saw the concern in Richard's eyes. Although he didn't reckon that explaining would gain them an ally, he reckoned knowing the truth might make Pierre's men worry about Murdock being with them.

So he told them about their history with Murdock, which made Richard nod.

'But now for some reason Winslow Scott has dropped the charges against him and he's been let out of jail,' Nicholson said, completing the story.

Richard sat in contemplative silence looking at the water.

'It doesn't seem that odd to me,' Richard said. 'After all, there was never any evidence to prove Murdock stole the lumber company's property or that he harmed the outlaw Chadwick Jackson.'

Nicholson glanced along the bank at Murdock, who was looking across the river. Several other men including Pierre were watching them, suggesting they knew Richard was getting the full story of their previous encounter with Murdock.

'I guess that's always been the problem. There was no good reason for Murdock to have the stolen property, and Chadwick wasn't in the rat-infested homestead where we found Murdock.'

Richard nodded. 'If Murdock killed Chadwick, his body would have turned up by now.'

'I doubt it.' Nicholson looked at Grantham, who provided a grim smile. 'The rumour is that Murdock cut his body into pieces that were so small, he was able to feed them to the rats.'

CHAPTER 10

'I haven't been to Pegasus Heights before,' Elmina said, her tone sad as she lowered her head. 'But I was supposed to come here with Igor Rodgers, the man who was delivering supplies to the Pegasus Lumber Company.'

'And you planned to help him steal the supplies?' Jim asked.

'No matter what I've said about you, I reckon you're not as big an idiot as you look,' she said, raising her head and regaining some of her usual feistiness. 'You can work it out.'

Jim walked to the edge of the rock to look down at their wagon.

From here, between gaps in the hills, he could see most of the way towards the trading post and he even caught a glimpse of reflected light, presumably from the railroad tracks.

'You've never been interested in my mission to find the supplies,' he said as he walked back to her while piecing together the situation. 'But then again, I find it hard to believe that anyone would be particularly concerned about some food going missing.'

She nodded and uttered a long sigh. 'I'm surprised it's taken you this long to figure that out.'

Jim nodded. 'So am I, but that means something else was on that supply wagon that was valuable, and that's what's got everyone excited.'

'Sure, and that leads me back to the original reason I hired you. I want you to find Pegasus for me.'

'I don't know what was on that supply wagon, but I'm sure it wasn't a winged horse.'

'Except there's two of them on the wagon, and others are on the crates.'

She pointed at the carved emblem emblazoned on the side of the wagon, and that made Jim smile.

'So you want something that emblem represents, and you never actually believed we'd find a real flying horse?'

She furrowed her brow and shook her head in disbelief.

'Of course not! I can't believe that you thought we were looking for a live flying horse.' She set her hands on her hips. 'Just when I was starting to think you were being perceptive, you prove me wrong again.'

'I never believed either that we were . . .' Jim trailed off when she gave him a thin smile. 'So what does that emblem represent?'

She softened her expression and then moved away

to stand on the edge of the outcrop looking to the hills.

'My father was one of the original owners of the Pegasus Lumber Company along with Winslow Scott. He died two years ago, but I never received my share of his inheritance. When I came to Beaver Ridge to find out why, my lawyer found out that when my father's health was failing, Winslow tricked him out of his share of the company.'

'So what did you do?'

'There was nothing I could do to claim my share of the company, but I had another option. When Winslow and my father started the company ten years ago, they had a golden horse made in the shape of the emblem.'

She gestured, signifying its shape as being around a foot long and flat.

'Ah!' Jim said as he finally heard something that made sense. He joined her and looked to the north.

'I figured that I'd settle for getting my hands on that golden horse. I hired a low-life Chadwick Jackson to find out what had happened to it and he created plenty of problems for the company, but he didn't help my quest none. So I hired Igor Rodgers instead with the instruction that he should act in a more subtle manner.'

'And Igor used the ruse of delivering supplies to the company to investigate and find out where Winslow had secreted the horse?'

'He did. He sent me a message to say that Winslow had buried it and he'd found the location. When he

80

made his next delivery, he planned to dig it up.' She frowned. 'But before I met up with you, I came across his dead body, and I now know where his wagon ended up, but I don't know what happened to the golden horse.'

Jim reckoned that if the horse had been in the wagon, it would now be long gone and so he walked past her to consider the wagon. Its presence suggested that one aspect of Archibald's original story was true, no matter how bizarre the presence of an intact wagon, on the top of an outcrop, in the middle of a lake was.

'Your father and Winslow Scott started the company ten years ago, and the prospector and his gold went missing ten years ago, too.'

She sighed. 'There's no need to say it. It's likely that my father and Winslow were the men who came across the prospector. They probably killed him. Then they used some of his gold to start the company, while they used the rest to make the golden horse.'

Jim frowned. 'Which means you're trying to claim something that your father stole in the first place.'

'I can't change the past, but that's why I've always wanted to find out the truth behind the legend of what happened at Pegasus Heights ten years ago. My father was a good man and Winslow Scott isn't. If one of them killed the prospector, I hope it was Winslow.'

Jim nodded and then turned to her to find she'd raised an eyebrow in a silent question.

'I promised to help you on your quest to find a

flying horse,' he said. 'Even though the quest has now changed to finding a golden flying horse, I'll still fulfil my promise. I also aim to find out enough about what's going on here to satisfy Marshal Collier so I can get my property back.'

'I'm obliged for your honesty, but it'll be hard to achieve both aims.'

'I'm not so sure.' He patted the side of the wagon and noted his hand felt damp. 'Because even though there's two mysteries here separated by ten years, I'm starting to think that there's only one solution.'

CHAPTER 11

Archibald Brown's trading post was having a lively night.

Dozens of horses were outside and from several hundred yards away, Nicholson had heard the animated chatter from inside.

Pierre entered the building with his men close behind him. Once inside, they milled around with the customers and fought their way to the counter.

Grantham informed Nicholson that the men all worked for the Pegasus Lumber Company. The main camp was several hours' riding away, but the excited chatter showed these men reckoned the journey was worthwhile.

Pierre reached the front where he waited for Archibald to notice him, his foot tapping on the floor being the only sign of his mounting irritation.

'Sorry,' Archibald said after serving four men with beer. 'There're double the usual numbers here tonight.'

'I can see you're busy,' Pierre said, 'So you'll be

pleased to hear I only want information.'

'The going rate for information today is five dollars.'

Pierre slapped a dollar in small change on the counter.

'As you've already told me one of the things I want to know for nothing, I'll pay a dollar to know where the man who paid you five dollars went.'

'That man was a decent fellow who honoured his deals. I won't sell him out for a dollar,' Archibald pushed the coins aside. 'I want five dollars.'

Pierre scowled, but when Archibald merely glared at him, he rummaged in his pocket.

Nicholson had experienced this routine before and he knew Pierre would negotiate by firstly providing only another dollar, but his hand had yet to emerge when Archibald flinched and looked past Pierre.

Murdock was striding purposefully towards the counter making the customers jostle and push to get out of his way.

Unfortunately, two men at the counter didn't notice his coming and so he shoved one man aside with a contemptuous lunge. Then he clamped a hand on the second man's shoulder and jerked him backwards.

Murdock then made short work of their jug of ale, making Pierre laugh.

'The sooner you accept my generous offer and tell me about Jim Dragon,' he said, 'the sooner we'll be on our way.'

Archibald winced. Then, with a faltering voice and his nervous gaze set on Murdock, he told Pierre about Jim along with his interest in the missing supplies.

Murdock's actions had already silenced the lumber men, most of whom presumably knew him from when he'd been a company guard, and the mention of the missing supplies made them shoot aggrieved glances at each other.

Nicholson caught Grantham's eye and the two men edged away from Murdock. Since Murdock had joined the group, Pierre's men had been less antagonistic towards them and they didn't complain when they slipped into their midst.

'There's going to be trouble,' Richard Clancy said.

'There always is when Murdock's around,' Nicholson said.

At the counter, Archibald finished his story while the men Murdock had barged aside moved in to surround him.

'At least Murdock is on our side,' Richard said.

'The only side Murdock's on is his own,' Grantham said. 'And that won't matter none when—'

He broke off when a chair went spinning across the post and broke apart on the counter beside Murdock. In a moment, Murdock grabbed a chair leg and swung round with it raised as a cudgel.

He smashed it down on the head of the nearest man, but before he could look for his next target, a mass of workers slammed into him and trapped him against the bar.

Within moments, chaos reigned.

While Pierre's men hurried towards Pierre, Nicholson and Grantham backed away towards the door. Several men moved between Nicholson and the door while Grantham was floored by a man who leapt on his back.

Seeing no other choice but to fight, Nicholson waded into the fray. He threw a punch at one man, the blow slamming into his cheek and knocking him over on to his back.

Then he threw a second punch at another man, but someone barged into him knocking the intended blow aside and making him hit the arm of another man.

This man appeared to think the man standing behind him had hit him as he turned on his heel and leapt at his presumed opponent. This opened up space between Nicholson and the door.

Nicholson looked for Grantham, but he'd disappeared behind the heaving mass of men. Beyond them, Pierre's men had surrounded their boss and they were confronting all-comers while Murdock was taking on at least four men alone.

One man held on to each arm and tried to drag Murdock's massive fists down while two other men grabbed his hips and tried to manhandle him over the counter. The fourth man knelt on the counter and wrapped an arm around Murdock's neck while he tried to push him down.

Nicholson noted that they were failing to move Murdock, but then a blow slammed into the back of his neck knocking him to his knees. Nicholson put a hand to the floor to lever himself up and then screeched when a heel crushed his fingers.

He yanked the hand away as knees and boots hammered against his side making him struggle to rise. He doubted the blows had been intended for him, but that was no comfort as he was battered down on to his front.

Then someone walked over him and another man even stood on his back and jerked around as, presumably, he carried on fighting.

Nicholson reckoned he had to get up now or he'd never get off the floor, and so he flexed his hands and shoved upwards. The man stumbled from his back and as he fell, he took down several other men.

Through the forest of legs, Nicholson then saw Grantham crawling along. He hailed him and after his third shout, Grantham turned to him.

'The door,' Grantham said, pointing. Then he set off crawling in a determined way in spite of the men who barged into him.

Nicholson reckoned that was the best way to act, although he stood up and, with his head down and his shoulders hunched, he moved on.

Blows thudded into his side and one crunched into his cheek, but he kept moving. All he could see ahead were whirling fists and men swaying as if they were weeds responding to a river current.

With a stumbling gait he emerged from the mass of seething humanity a few feet from the door. He looked down as Grantham appeared, although such was his determination, he crawled on until his fore-head tapped against the wall.

Grantham jumped to his feet, picked out Nicholson with a smile, and turned to the door. Nicholson followed him, but then the door was flung open and the boss of the lumber company, Winslow Scott, strode in.

Three men were at his shoulders and they surveyed the fight inside with the jaundiced eyes of men who dealt with trouble daily. Winslow nodded and one man thrust a six-shooter high.

He fired, and then fired again until he'd gathered the fighting men's attentions. The moment they saw who had arrived the workers ceased their activities.

With nobody moving, Pierre slipped through the crowded room to stand before Winslow.

'I am Pierre Dulaine,' he declared. 'And I demand an apology for your men's unacceptable behaviour.'

Winslow snorted. 'Nobody demands anything of me, but I do demand explanations. I'll start with the most responsible man here, and that's not you.'

Pierre bristled, but Winslow looked at Archibald, who came out from behind the counter where he had taken refuge.

'These men asked too many questions, including about the missing supplies,' he said, gesturing at Pierre.

Grumbling sounded around the room until Winslow beckoned for calm.

'We know you're angry and we're working to ensure you're all fed.'

Winslow looked at Pierre, silently giving him the opportunity to calm the situation down. Accordingly, Pierre raised his chin and put a hand to his heart.

'I only wish to help the unfortunate victims of that most heinous crime,' he declared. 'I am skilled in the art of finding things that others can't and I am at your service.'

Nicholson tensed, but the beating he reckoned Pierre deserved for his untruths failed to materialize and instead, a ripple of nodding drifted around the room.

'If you know the supplies passed by, you have as much information as I have,' Winslow said.

'That's all I needed to know,' Pierre said with a bow. 'With your permission, we'll resume our search, although if you should come across Jim Dragon, you would do well to detain him.'

Winslow didn't reply and so Pierre moved on to the door, but Archibald raised a hand.

'A woman called Elmina Fay has joined up with Jim Dragon,' he called.

Nicholson looked at Pierre to find he was turning to him, as both men shared a rare moment in which their thoughts coincided.

Elmina's intervention during the confrontation with Jim Dragon outside Beaver Ridge had seemed odd at the time, and she had been evasive about her reason for being there.

Before either of them could speak up, Winslow made the connection.

'It sounds as if we should have a word with Jim

Dragon and Elmina Fay,' he said.

Archibald started to agree, but his comment was drowned out as Winslow's declaration forged common cause amongst the previously warring workers.

Winslow backed away and Pierre was carried along to the door, except this time with everyone slapping him on the back and asking him for more information about Jim.

Nicholson and Grantham side-stepped to let everyone leave first, but Nicholson wished he'd joined the fray when Murdock loomed up before them.

'So it seems that our numbers have swelled,' Murdock said.

'They have, but mainly with people you had been trying to beat to a pulp,' Nicholson said.

'Maybe, but that's sure to lead to chaos,' Murdock laughed. 'And the thing about chaos is, people can get killed and nobody will ever notice.'

CHAPTER 12

'It's too dark to find anything now,' Elmina said. 'Give up until tomorrow.'

She was right, but as Jim had no idea what they should look for come sun-up, he wanted to use every scrap of light to give him ideas to sleep on.

He put a hand to his brow to shield his eyes from the low arc of twilight on the horizon and looked across the rippling water of the lake.

Earlier, they'd rowed back from Pegasus Heights with the current aiding them on the return journey. Then he and Elmina had climbed to the top of the rise that they had travelled around in approaching the lake.

With better light he would be able to look down on the wagon sitting on the outcrop. Although he was starting to think that even if he stood here until their supplies ran out, he'd never think of a reason why it should be there.

To take his mind off the dilemma, and to avoid having to admit to Elmina that she was right, he turned to look towards the railroad where he saw more lights than he'd expected to see. They were moving and, now that he'd noticed them, he also realized that for a while he'd heard the low susurration of people talking.

'What do you make of that?' he asked, beckoning Elmina to join him.

'There are a few homesteads around Pegasus Heights, but not that many people,' she said, considering what was now clearly around thirty riders with many of them holding brands aloft. 'They must be mighty interested in something for them to come out here. We need to find out what it is.'

Jim shook his head. 'We'll stay up here. In my experience, a lot of people gathering outside at night usually means trouble.'

'Your experience has failed to help us find anything. These people stand more chance of working out where we can start than you have.'

Jim couldn't think of a retort to that and so he stayed quiet as she looked for a way down, although as the twilight was on the lake side of the hill, she soon turned to go back to their wagon.

The riders were now coming around the base of the hill, but as he thought she was probably right, he stayed to consider Pegasus Heights, which in the last few minutes had become even harder to see.

In the hope that the deadline caused by the new people arriving might force him to have an idea, he peered at the natural bowl around the lake, but he only confirmed the hills were broadly of the same height.

He set off after her, wondering if that observation told him anything. He had to move slowly as the going was treacherous.

Elmina had already reached the bottom and he could just make out her outline. She was standing by their wagon waving at the riders as they crested the pass between the hills.

Her intervention made the lead riders speed up, while those in the middle spread out and the riders bringing up the rear stopped. Their odd behaviour gave Jim a twinge of concern and he tried to attract Elmina's attention with a wave.

He couldn't tell if she'd seen him and as he didn't want to alert the newcomers to his presence, he ducked down. Then he made his cautious way down the slope while taking advantage of any cover the terrain provided.

He was halfway down the hill when the lead riders reached Elmina.

'Would you be Elmina Fay?' one man called.

'I sure am,' Elmina said. She considered him. 'And I know all about you. You're Winslow Scott, the owner of the . . .'

She trailed off and a moment later, one of the riders carrying a brand came close enough for Jim to see that several riders had drawn guns and aimed them at her.

'You're coming with me,' Winslow said, 'But only after you've told me where your accomplice is.'

'I don't have an. . . .' She stepped forward with her customary air of confidence. 'You'll tell me what this is about or you'll regret it.'

Up the hill, Jim reckoned that if he made his presence known he would only enflame an already fraught situation and so he hunkered down to watch developments.

'Igor Rodgers was killed,' Winslow said. 'You're the last person known to have been with him.'

'And you know where our supplies are,' another rider said before she could reply.

She shook her head. 'I'm not responsible for either of those mishaps. As I'm sure Archibald Brown told you, I'm out here looking for a flying horse.'

Winslow laughed and this started a ripple of derision.

'That's the worst excuse I've ever heard. You'll come with me.'

Elmina started to shout more demands, but they were drowned out as the group surrounded her.

With Winslow having around twenty men with him, Jim reckoned any rescue attempt he might mount would be even less successful than his first attempt to rescue her had been.

So instead, he watched them take her away. As they did that, he kept his head down as the group moved back towards the crest of the hill.

Then, under the cover of darkness, he worked his way back up the slope so he could watch where they took her, but he'd yet to reach the top when he noticed that some of the group had stayed.

Several men were standing at the edge of the water. Some of them were watching the mob head off to the north, but most of the men were peering across the water at Pegasus Heights while one man had found the raft Jim had built earlier.

This man directed two others to find out if it could be used. When he shook his hands, as if in disgust at having touched the filthy and damp wood, Jim smiled.

'So Pierre Dulaine has finally arrived,' he said to himself, 'And as always, he's ten steps behind me.'

Then he moved on to follow Elmina.

CHAPTER 13

'I'm leaving you in charge,' Pierre said breezily to Richard Clancy.

'I'd prefer to come with you,' Richard said with a worried glance at Murdock.

Pierre picked a dry spot on the raft and settled down.

'I need someone I can trust back here.' He pointed at Nicholson and Grantham and then at Murdock. 'Keep them from leaving and keep him from killing them.'

Pierre's men laughed before they set about working out how to steer the raft away from the side.

'You won't give me any trouble, will you?' Richard asked Nicholson and Grantham when the raft reached the halfway point to Pegasus Heights.

'We won't,' Nicholson said with a pointed look at Murdock, who ignored them and watched the raft move away. Then he joined Grantham in sitting down.

Presently, Pierre disappeared from view into the

shadowy area beneath the outcrop and shortly after that, curses and thuds sounded as the men clearly struggled to get off the raft.

'He should have waited until morning,' Richard said with a sorry shake of the head.

'He's worried that Jim Dragon's ahead of him,' Nicholson said.

'From what I've seen, Jim's always ahead of him, which means the supplies aren't here, even if the wagon is.'

Nicholson grunted that he agreed while Grantham nodded, but Nicholson hadn't expected that Murdock would start laughing. The sound was deep and throaty, as if he had genuinely found their conversation amusing rather than that he was trying to disconcert them.

'The supplies aren't here,' he said. 'They never were.'

Nicholson and Grantham didn't respond, leaving Richard to ask the obvious question.

'How do you know that?'

'Because Winslow told me just before he got me out of jail.'

Richard frowned. 'Which begs the question, why did he do that?'

'Because something valuable has gone missing and he reckons I'm the right man to find it.'

Richard lowered his head, seemingly lost for words.

'Why did you have to ask?' Grantham murmured with a groan.

Murdock looked at Richard, and Richard confirmed that he'd noticed the danger he was in when he jerked away. With surprising speed for a large man, Murdock advanced on him. In three long paces, he'd reached Richard and while still moving on, he clubbed him about the side of the head with a massive forearm.

Richard slammed down on his side at the water's edge where he tried to raise himself before with a groan he flopped back down. Nicholson and Grantham then got to their feet, and when Murdock advanced on them, they stepped backwards.

'What's gone missing that's so valuable it made Winslow help you?' Nicholson asked, purely to keep Murdock talking in the hope of buying them time.

'Dead men don't need to know that,' Murdock said.

With that, Murdock charged at them. Even having seen how fast he moved, his speed took Nicholson by surprise.

He and Grantham separated with Grantham running towards the water and Nicholson heading away. Murdock spread his huge arms, but he still failed to grab either man and he passed between them.

His failure didn't appear to concern him, as when he turned back to them, his eyes were lively as he clearly anticipated the fight to come.

Richard was stirring, but Nicholson doubted he'd be able to gather his wits in time to help them. So he and Grantham spread out to stand on either side of Murdock.

Grantham had his back to the water reducing his escape routes and so Murdock swung round to face him. He crouched forward and spread his arms as he advanced on him.

Grantham glanced at the lake. With a shake of the head he dismissed the thought of seeking escape in the bone-chilling water and moved to the left.

Murdock followed him with his arms, but Grantham's move had been only a feint and he leapt to the right. Murdock checked himself, but he wasn't fast enough to waylay Grantham as, bent double, he scrambled away.

Grantham managed a few paces before he slipped on the slimy ground beside the water and went all his length.

With a roar of delight Murdock stomped three long paces to loom over Grantham. He waited until Grantham looked up and saw how hopeless his situation was before he hammered both hands down on his back.

Without any discernible strain he raised Grantham off the ground, swung him backward to gain leverage, and then launched him forward.

A cry of alarm escaped Grantham's lips as he crashed to the ground on his chest ten feet away and then somersaulted twice before he came to a halt lying curled up.

Gingerly, he got to his knees, but he was still too shaken to gain his feet and instead, he slumped down to lie on his side.

Murdock lumbered towards him with his hands

raised ready to repeat the treatment, and so Nicholson put his head down and charged at him. Murdock heard him coming and he swung round to stand before him.

With a leading shoulder Nicholson ran into Murdock's chest, and he came to a jarring halt before rebounding to lie on his back at Murdock's feet. With Grantham lying a few feet away, Murdock grinned.

He slapped a meaty hand down on Nicholson's shoulder and dragged him towards Grantham where he repeated the movement with Grantham. Then he drew both men up to their feet.

'Tell us the truth about what you're looking for,' Grantham said, his voice low and faltering.

'You're trying to buy time,' Murdock said. 'That won't do you no good because I intend to take my time over this.'

He licked his lips while squeezing each man's shoulder. They both braced themselves and then tried to tear themselves away from his hands.

Grantham thrust his head forward and drew himself closer to Murdock before aiming frantic kicks at Murdock's legs, while Nicholson put a hand over Murdock's hand and with a tug he managed to raise it.

Nicholson's delight was short-lived when he found that Murdock had moved on his own volition so that he could clamp his hand around his throat. Murdock repeated the same treatment with Grantham without apparently registering that Grantham was kicking him.

'We can help you—' Nicholson said before Murdock squeezed his throat and cut off his plea.

'Don't beg and don't fight back,' Murdock said. He flared his eyes. 'It'll just make me angry.'

Murdock chuckled. Then his eyes narrowed as if he'd gathered enough enjoyment out of their distress and he raised his arms.

Nicholson threw both hands to the hand wrapped around his throat, but the fingers were like bands of steel as they tightened, cutting off his windpipe while his feet dangled in the air.

His vision darkened until all he could see was Murdock's smiling face gleaming in the moonlight while another gleaming object seemed to hover behind his head.

Grantham gasped something, but the words wouldn't form and so Nicholson concentrated on the object, trying to work out what it was in the hope that the effort might keep him conscious.

The object moved, letting Nicholson see that it was a log and that Richard was brandishing it. Murdock didn't react to Richard sneaking up on him from behind and he continued to squeeze.

With his vision dimming Nicholson watched Richard swing the log, and it slammed into the back of Murdock's head with a dull thud. The log broke in two.

His vision blackened and the next he knew his shoulder was being shaken. Vaguely he batted the tormentor away, but the movement showed him that he was no longer being strangled, so he raised his head to find Grantham was trying to rouse him.

Behind him stood Richard while further away lay Murdock's body.

'It took two swipes,' Richard said. 'But he went down in the end.'

'I'm obliged,' Nicholson croaked before feeling his throat. Then he looked around, weighing up his chances of getting away before Murdock regained consciousness.

Grantham acknowledged his intent with a frown and pointed at the water. So Nicholson raised himself and then wished he hadn't.

Pierre was stepping off the raft and, as Murdock had promised, he didn't look happy. He scowled as he moved up the slope while he worried at the damp patches on his clothes.

He brightened only when he saw the comatose Murdock and the three bedraggled men.

'I'm pleased to see that you managed to amuse yourself while I was away,' he said.

CHAPTER 14

Elmina's interrogation appeared to be over, and her lowered head as she was led back to her tent suggested the outcome had been a troubling one.

Last night, Jim had followed Winslow Scott and the lumber men. They had headed north for an hour, keeping beside the creek that fed into the lake until they'd reached their encampment.

Jim had settled down on high ground to await developments, but after Winslow had put Elmina in a tent on the edge of the camp and placed two guards outside, he had then settled down for the night.

This morning, she'd been led away to a log cabin where Winslow and several other men gathered.

Jim presumed she'd been questioned, but before he could get too concerned, she'd been allowed to leave. Then she'd again been left alone with only the two guards standing outside her tent.

So Jim started planning his next move.

Trees surrounded the camp on three sides with

only the area beside the creek having been cleared. Here, the ground fell away sharply and the creek would have created a waterfall, but a dam had reduced the water flow downstream to a trickle.

Jim presumed they'd done this to aid their operations and it explained why the creek wasn't substantial enough to fill such a large lake.

He figured that as long as he didn't approach the camp along the cleared area, he could use the cover of the trees to get within thirty yards of her tent. Even so, with the many men milling about, he doubted he could cover even that short distance without being seen.

Thankfully, as the sun rose above the trees, the workers got ready to move out. They gathered by the dam and then walked across it gingerly in single-file before heading to a corral.

Over the next hour, most of them moved off on a variety of wagons through the trees heading north and out of sight.

When only a dozen or so men were left in the camp, Jim worked his way closer to the edge of the clear area on a path that kept a few trees between him and open space. He reached a tree opposite the side of Elmina's tent without incident, leaving him to watch the guards.

As they were guarding a seemingly docile woman in an isolated camp, the men mooched around displaying their boredom openly, presumably in the hope that someone would relieve them.

While they were being inattentive, Jim moved on

along a circuitous route that kept the guards out of sight until he reached the back of the tent.

He caught his breath while ensuring that in this position he couldn't be seen. Then, using a knife, he quickly sliced through the canvas to create a gap.

He slipped inside to find Elmina sitting cross-legged on the ground facing him.

'I've been wondering when you'd get here,' she said with a sigh. 'It took even longer than I thought.'

'Be quiet,' Jim whispered, putting a finger to his lips for emphasis.

'If my guards didn't hear you blundering your way in here, they won't hear me speaking to you, will they?'

Jim reckoned anything he said would only encourage her to speak again and so he moved past her to the tent flap. For several moments he listened and as it was silent outside, he turned back to her and gestured at the slit in the canvas.

'Now,' he mouthed.

She considered him with her lips upturned with wry amusement, but she made no move to leave, while outside one of the guards spoke up. Jim couldn't hear what he said and it didn't sound as if he was concerned, but that was enough for him.

He returned a wry smile of his own while walking over to her. Then, giving her no opportunity to argue, he slapped a hand over her mouth, drew her to her feet, and marched her away.

He reached the gap before she started struggling, but he'd gathered firm holds of her jaw and of her right shoulder and he manoeuvred her outside with ease. He paused to check nobody was visible nearby, which gave her enough time to flash him a warning glare.

As he couldn't tell whether she was trying to convey that she wanted to speak or that she would leave willingly now, he kept hold of her and moved off to the trees.

He didn't stop until they'd walked past several trees to reach a position where the trunks would provide them with cover from anyone who happened to look their way.

He positioned her behind a tree and glanced at the tent, confirming the guards were still patrolling. Then he moved in front of her so he could look into her eyes.

When she nodded, he removed his hand, although he kept it raised as a warning that he would silence her again if she didn't co-operate.

'Why?' she said using a level tone.

'Because I'm rescuing you.'

'We've already established that rescuing is a task you're poor at. I hired you to solve the mystery of where the flying horse went, not to rescue me.' She slapped her hands on her hips. 'And especially when I didn't need rescuing, again!'

She'd raised her voice making Jim peer past her at the camp. Sure enough, the guards were now conferring.

Through the trees, he could see them only intermittently, but there was no mistaking the result of their debate when they looked into Elmina's tent.

'Perhaps you didn't,' Jim said, 'but you do now.'

He grabbed her arm and moved to leave, but she dug in her heels. For several moments they strained to go in opposite directions until he adopted his policy in the tent of not giving her an option.

With one hand clutching her hip and the other clamped around her upper arm, he hoisted her off the ground. Then, with her bent over a shoulder, he turned away from the tent from which sounds of consternation were emerging.

Within moments, the guards had raised the alarm and this time she didn't complain as he returned along the path he'd taken to reach the tent. With the effort involved in manoeuvring himself and her through the trees, he found the going slow and he'd yet to draw level with the dam when men started scurrying around reducing their chances of reaching safety unnoticed.

'Put me down,' she said with an irritated tone while wriggling. 'Then we might get to where we're going before anyone stops us getting there.'

He stopped. 'Only if you promise to stop fighting me.'

'You've given me no choice.' She stopped wriggling and so he put her back down on the ground. 'I was doing fine before you turned up. I'd gained Winslow's trust and with a little more delving I might have found out where the golden horse is, but I won't now, will I?'

'Why didn't you just tell me that back in the tent

instead of complaining?'

'I would have told you everything if you hadn't slapped a hand over my mouth.'

'If I hadn't . . .' Jim trailed off and looked skyward, reckoning that if he tried to win this argument, they'd still be standing here when they were discovered. 'We need to get away while we still can.'

'Then leave it to me.' She looked around. 'I'm practiced at rescuing idiots in distress.'

Jim gestured, inviting her to lead the way, but instead of continuing up the slope and back to the wagon, she looked across the clearing at the dam. Then she set off and within moments, she had moved clear of the trees.

Jim thought her reckless action was inviting capture, but when he looked at the camp, Winslow had gathered everyone around him and he was delivering his orders.

Nobody was looking their way, and so before the search got underway, he hurried after her. He reached her at the spot by the dam where she'd hunkered down behind a felled tree.

'They're sure to find us in such an obvious place,' he said.

'They might, but we won't be here by the time they come up here.' She pointed across the dam. 'We were sure to be seen if we'd tried to get away on your wagon, but they'll find it before too much longer and while that distracts them, we'll go elsewhere.'

'Afoot?'

She shook her head. 'They've left some horses on

the other side of the river.'

Jim nodded approvingly. 'You seem to have found out a lot in a short time here.'

'It doesn't take much to be more observant than you've been,' she said before moving off.

He followed her on to the dam. She walked along a log that was below the level that was visible from the camp, although Jim had to walk hunched over to ensure he remained hidden.

The water was thirty feet below him, while through gaps between the logs he saw the water on the other side was as high as the log on which they were walking. The dam had been constructed crudely and so the wood was slippery, forcing them to move slowly.

They were halfway across when from the camp shouting sounded as the pursuit got underway. The noise made Elmina raise herself and she nodded approvingly when she noted the pursuers wouldn't pass the dam before they reached the other side.

Moving to the corral and securing mounts on which to leave while remaining unseen wouldn't be easy as it was on the opposite side of the creek to the camp. But he judged Elmina had the right idea that when the loggers discovered his wagon, the distraction might help them.

Feeling more optimistic, he put his back to the high logs and while walking sideways after Elmina he looked downstream. He considered the journey back to the lake and the unsolved mystery of the wagon on the top of Pegasus Heights.

He came to a sudden halt and he must have uttered an exclamation of surprise without realizing it as Elmina stopped and shot him an irritated look. She beckoned him to hurry up, but he shook his head.

'Damn,' he said.

'Yes, it's a dam,' she said. 'And if we don't get off it in the next minute, we'll be caught.'

'I said "damn", but I guess I meant dam, too.' He pointed downstream when she furrowed her brow. 'I've figured it out. I know how the trick that's been played on us and on Archibald ten years ago was done.'

'I'm pleased for you. Now, hurry up or you'll never get the chance to do anything about it.'

Jim nodded and while still peering downstream in wonderment that he hadn't worked it out beforehand, he hurried along the dam. He joined her as she stepped on to dry land where she peered around the logs at the corral.

He looked over her shoulder and confirmed nobody was visible on their side, but on the other side, Winslow was leading half of the camp beside the creek while the other half headed into the trees.

The latter group would be sure to find the wagon within a few minutes and so they hunkered down beneath two overhanging logs to await developments.

He expected she'd now ask him for an explanation, but she said nothing and so he slapped the nearest logs.

110

'This dam keeps the water back and that's reducing the amount of water that reaches the lake.'

He looked at her triumphantly, but she only shrugged.

'So you're saying that when they release the dam, that creates a surge of water that could have temporarily raised the water level on the lake and taken the wagon up on to the outcrop?'

'Sure,' he said, her monotone delivery deflating his excitement in resolving the mystery.

She frowned. 'There wouldn't be enough water and besides, that doesn't answer the bigger question of what happened to the people who were using the wagons.'

'I reckon there is enough water and the interesting thing is why something twice went missing when the dam was breached.'

'I accept that the water could have risen the second time, but ten years ago there wasn't a dam here.'

'I'd forgotten that,' Jim murmured, still feeling unwilling to abandon his theory. 'But the water could still have risen ten years ago for some other reason.'

'It could have, but you've not figured anything out yet.' She raised a hand when he started to object. 'And be quiet. Winslow will hear you.'

To avoid getting irritated by her lack of enthusiasm, he peered through a gap in the logs and saw that Elmina was right.

Winslow was now close-by. He was standing on the other side of the dam while ordering others to spread out and look in all directions.

When everyone was in position, he moved on to the dam.

'Trouble,' Jim whispered.

Elmina didn't need to ask what was happening and she joined him in judging how long they'd take to secure horses. Without conferring with him she moved off slowly while keeping low as she tried to get as far as possible without being noticed.

Jim fell in behind her as they worked their way around the edge of the dam, but when they reached the corner she jerked back and shook her head.

'Too many people are watching,' she said. 'We'll just have to make a run for it.'

She considered him, clearly for once giving him a chance to offer an alternative, and so he glanced around.

With his thoughts still on his solution to the mystery, he noted ropes around the logs that held them in place, and sticking out of one log was a machete that was presumably used to trim small branches.

He reached around the corner of the dam and secured the machete. When she looked at him in bemusement, he brandished the long blade and then, not giving her a chance to pour cold water on his reckless idea, he doubled back.

At the other corner, he watched Winslow approach. When Winslow was at the halfway point across the dam, he stood up and stepped into view, although he kept the machete hidden behind a log.

'Stay back,' he shouted. 'We're leaving now and we don't want no trouble.'

Winslow stopped and considered him. 'Elmina Fay is going nowhere until I have the answers I need.'

'I'd hoped you wouldn't say that.' He raised the machete and then felt his shark's tooth. 'Let us leave, or I'll destroy your dam and you with it. You have thirty seconds to comply.'

Winslow shook his head while laughing. 'That's a pathetic threat. It'd take the whole camp all day to cause any damage to this dam. Put down the machete or someone will shoot you. You have ten seconds to comply.'

Winslow's confident tone made Jim lower the machete, while behind him Elmina muttered to herself in irritation. A flash of anger quickened his heart and so he picked out a rope at water level that looked like it was holding an important log in place.

He raised the blade high and sliced it down on the rope. The tension in the rope was high and the rope split and snaked away and so heartened, he repeated the action on two more loops of rope that he could reach without venturing on to the dam.

He picked out another rope, but he paused with the machete held above it and looked at Winslow. His hopes that he might have shocked him into relenting fled as Winslow was looking at him with bemusement.

Worse, the logs that he'd released still sat firmly in the same place and they showed no sign that they might fall away.

'What now?' Elmina said at his shoulder.

Jim slammed the machete down over the loop of rope and then left the blade buried in the wood.

'Run!' he said.

CHAPTER 15

'I assume we'll try to find out where Jim Dragon's gone,' Nicholson said.

'I'll no longer follow two steps behind that man,' Pierre said. 'I'll figure this out for myself and get to the supplies first.'

This claim made Murdock pay attention to proceedings for the first time since he'd regained consciousness late last night. He contented himself with glaring across the campsite at Nicholson, but unlike the previous times he'd done that, Nicholson had no trouble meeting his gaze.

Last night, Murdock had revealed information that they could use against him, if he were to act threateningly again. That option was still available as strangely, Richard hadn't divulged this information to Pierre.

This failing had surprised Nicholson, but the group had stayed close together. So he hadn't had the chance to ask him what he hoped to gain by keeping secret the fact that Murdock was following

Winslow's instructions to look for something.

'I don't reckon you're likely to figure anything out,' Nicholson said, hoping his comment would provoke a reaction from Richard or Murdock, but it was Pierre who grunted with anger.

'Your usefulness ended when you led me to the trading post,' he said. 'Unless you can come up with another good idea, I'll no longer have a use for you.'

Pierre shot a meaningful glance at Murdock, but Nicholson set his hands on his hips.

'If you're not prepared to follow Jim, you should follow Elmina.'

'Why?'

Nicholson struggled to find an answer, but Grantham spoke up.

'Because Winslow took her away to the logging camp in the north,' he said. 'And I reckon he's the key to all this.'

Pierre nodded slowly, and then turned to the north.

'If you're right, I'll be pleased. If you're wrong, I'll let you discuss the matter with Murdock.'

Pierre gestured for everyone to move out, although he cast a sideways glance at Richard, as if he expected him to explain what had happened last night.

Nicholson and Grantham ensured they stayed back to let Pierre take the lead, but so did Murdock.

'You should have told Pierre why you suspect Winslow,' Murdock said when Pierre had moved out of earshot.

'We still could,' Nicholson said, raising his chin with defiance. 'Three of us now know there's something valuable out there and that you're working for Winslow, not Pierre. You won't silence all of us.'

Murdock shook his head. 'I've spent three months dreaming about how I'd kill you when I got out of prison, but after last night, I'll settle for just ending your miserable existences the first chance I get.'

He considered both men and then jerked forward making them both scramble away, but his movement had been only a feint.

Murdock laughed before turning away to join Pierre in heading away.

Winslow's men were closing on them.

For the first two miles after leaving the camp, Jim and Elmina had made good time afoot, but now the strain of running downhill was taking its toll and they were both struggling for breath and to keep their footing.

Back at the camp, they'd had to abandon their attempt to reach the horses when Winslow's men had started shooting at them and their sustained gunfire had cut them off from the corral. So they'd turned and fled down the side of the creek taking a path where trees had been cleared away.

They'd been able to move out of sight quickly, but once Winslow and his men had moved over the dam, the pursuit had got underway.

With the route being tricky to navigate, the pursuit had also been on foot, but their pursuers knew the

117

terrain and they'd followed them with steady confidence.

Now, they were spreading out as they sought to round them up.

Despite that, the terrain was heavy on rocks, but light on trees – Jim had yet to see anywhere where they might hide and neither had he seen the lake.

Ahead, the slope petered out on to a flat section that continued for a hundred yards until the slope fell away again. Jim reckoned Winslow was planning to corner them there.

'We'll never get away from them,' Elmina said between gasps for breath.

'It took me only an hour to reach the camp,' Jim said. 'So I reckon it's not too much further to the lake.'

'It might not be, but there's nowhere to hole up there,' she yelled, her face reddening.

Getting angry with him again appeared to give Elmina a burst of strength. She drew ahead and hurried down the slope with her fists pumping as she tried to gather more speed, making Jim wonder what he should do to annoy her some more so they could keep moving quickly.

When she thundered down on to the flat section, she was moving so quickly she had to wheel her arms to keep her balance and Jim had the same problem when he followed her.

It took him a dozen strides before he was able to run upright, and when he looked over his shoulder, to his delight they'd drawn ahead of Winslow and his men, who were still moving steadily down the slope.

'If we can see the lake beyond the next drop, we have a chance,' he shouted after her.

She waved a dismissive hand at him, but she kept running suggesting that despite everything, his comments had given her hope.

He speeded up and drew level with her thirty yards from the edge where he tried to catch her eye to give her an encouraging smile, but when she turned to him her eyes were wide and worried.

'No chance,' she gasped.

He gestured over his shoulder, signifying that Winslow's men had only just reached the bottom of the slope, but she shook her head and nodded ahead. Getting her meaning, he peered beyond the edge and gulped.

The lake was visible for the first time, presenting a circular blue expanse that dominated the view.

He could see the protruding outcrop that from here made the lake look like an eye, but as more of the terrain became visible, it was clear they hadn't covered even half the journey.

Worse, the immediate land ahead was so devoid of features, their only hope of avoiding capture was to stay ahead of their pursuers, and Elmina's burst of speed was dying out at the same rate as her hope.

'At least we know how far we have to go,' Jim said, forcing a smile.

She breathed deeply before she could gather enough air into her lungs to reply.

'We do, but I can't make it.'

119

As she was slowing with every pace, Jim didn't argue.

'Then we make our stand here.'

'Only you're armed and we're facing a dozen armed men.'

Jim sighed with exasperation. 'Then we stand here while we catch our breath.'

'I can't stand any longer,' she murmured before proving she wasn't exaggerating by staggering on to the edge.

The moment she'd crested the edge, she flopped down to lie on her back on the slope. With her head below the ground level, she gasped for breath.

Jim followed her at a more sedate pace and stopped in a position where his upper body would be visible to Winslow. He drew his gun, although he kept it out of sight and faced back up the slope.

His action had an immediate effect when the pursuers slowed to a halt fifty yards away.

'Let us go and we won't give you no trouble,' Jim shouted, without much hope of success other than to give Elmina enough time to regain her breath.

'You've already given us enough trouble,' Winslow said, stepping forward. 'Elmina still has plenty of questions to answer, and I reckon so do you.'

'We can't help you find the flying horse. I know how the supply wagon got stranded on Pegasus Heights, and it sure didn't have nothing to do with Pegasus.'

Elmina shot him an irritated glance while Winslow shook his head. Then he gestured for his men to spread out.

Jim didn't want this confrontation to descend into a gunfight as Elmina had been right and they were unlikely to prevail, but with Winslow giving him no choice, he drew his gun into view. The men continued to move and so he fired high.

Everyone stopped. Then they flinched down while looking around in trepidation.

Jim hadn't expected such a fearful reaction and he had to smile, but his optimism died when Elmina sighed and shot him a disdainful look.

'You didn't scare them,' she said.

'Then what did?'

She raised a hand to her ear while sporting a puzzled expression, and when the men continued to look around, Jim strained his hearing. He heard a distant noise that sounded like a louder version of the water surging along in the creek beside them.

He shrugged and looked at her for suggestions.

'I don't know,' she said, 'but I reckon this is the distraction we've been hoping for.'

Keeping low, she moved away from the edge before resuming their journey down the slope. As she had yet to regain her breath and she moved slowly, Jim dallied to work out what had troubled Winslow's men.

They appeared to identify the source of the rumbling sound as coming from up the slope as they all turned their backs on him.

When he noticed that the water in the creek appeared to be higher and moving faster than when they'd settled down, he slapped his forehead. Then he stood up and joined the others in looking up the slope.

He couldn't see anything yet, but the water to his left was rising by the moment. Then Winslow turned away from the creek and broke into a run, and he headed away at a right angle to the water.

When his men followed, Jim reckoned he'd seen enough and he hurried after Elmina. Even in the few moments he'd been watching Winslow, the water height had increased again.

'So it seems that I destroyed the dam, after all,' he said to himself.

CHAPTER 16

The water in the creek had swelled to only fifty feet below them when Jim confirmed his worst fears about what had frightened Winslow.

The minor damage he'd caused to the dam earlier must have spread and now a wall of water was surging down the slope towards them. The loggers had clearly encountered such problems before and so they'd run away from the creek, but Elmina was still running beside the water.

He felt his shark's tooth, and then put on a burst of speed to join her.

'We have to do what Winslow did and move away from the creek,' Jim shouted.

'Stop talking,' Elmina said between pained intakes of breath. 'Keep running.'

'That won't do no good,' Jim gestured to the advancing water making Elmina look over her shoulder.

Her mouth opened in shock and she stomped to a halt. When she made no attempt to move away again,

Jim also stopped.

He looked again at the water. In the few moments since he'd last considered it, the deluge had spread out to cover the whole slope for several hundred yards on both sides of the creek.

He could no longer see Winslow's group, but even though Elmina had started running before those men had moved, he couldn't be sure they'd reach safety.

The leading extent of the wash of water was about to pound down on to the flat stretch of ground where they'd rested up briefly, and Jim judged it to be moving so fast it would overcome them in another minute.

Elmina got over her shock first and tugged his arm.

'Come on,' she murmured with a resigned tone. 'We have to try to outrun this.'

Jim felt equally resigned about their prospects, but in the hope that the further they ran, the more the water would lose its strength, he locked hands with her. Then, despite their tiredness, they pounded down the slope.

They leapt over rocks and skidded along sections of dirt. Even when one of them stumbled, the other one tugged to ensure they both kept running.

The noise grew to a deafening roar behind them making Jim look back.

The deluge had reached the edge of the flat area and its speed was great enough to send the water gushing dozens of feet into the air before it crashed

124

down to the ground and hurtled down the slope.

The sight made Jim's guts churn and he must have slowed down as Elmina yanked on his arm. He continued running, but he couldn't stop himself from watching the water loom ever closer.

The surging brown mass swept away the rocks and fallen trees in its path making Jim think the reason the slope was so barren was that deluges like this must have swept down to the lake before.

Confirmation of his theory about how the wagon had ended up on the outcrop didn't cheer him and neither did the sight of the debris the water was pushing along.

'We have to head to the creek,' he said, dragging her to the side. 'It's our only hope.'

She resisted. 'If the water doesn't kill us, all the debris in it surely will.'

'Perhaps, but at least we can control when we hit the water rather than waiting for it to hit us.'

She shot him a dubious and frightened look, but when he pulled her aside again she didn't resist.

He didn't need to say that he had no realistic expectation that his plan would work, but the moment they turned to the water, Jim saw one piece of debris he hadn't noticed before.

A wagon was swirling down the channel. Its open back was empty and it was riding high in the water.

'Riding that wagon to safety is the best idea you've ever had,' Elmina said with a wide grin.

Jim didn't think it was worth pointing out that he hadn't noticed it before and that its presence was down to luck. Instead, he joined her in taking a course that would intercept the wagon.

The top of the bank was fifty feet ahead while from the corner of his eye the advancing water was moving so quickly, he struggled to concentrate on it.

He did his best to ignore everything and moving on as quickly as possible and with his head down, he and Elmina ran on to the bank. When they crested the bank, the water was only ten feet below them and they'd moved ahead of the wagon.

He looked at her and she returned a nod. Then they both took two long strides and dived.

At the last moment they released hands and so Jim sliced into the water with greater ease than he'd expected. He swam forward for three strokes underwater before he came up and faced upriver.

Elmina had already breached the surface and she'd judged her dive into the water better than Jim had, as she'd come to a halt in the water along the path the wagon would take. Then, with firm strokes, she swam against the current and when the wagon loomed over her, she grabbed hold of a corner.

She glanced around, presumably looking for him, but the water was churning and she didn't appear to notice him. So she bobbed up in the water and grabbed the rim of the sideboard with both hands.

While Jim swam towards the wagon, she locked her elbows and rolled over the side to disappear from view. Heartened by her success, he swam with strong strokes towards the wagon, but with the water rising all the while he struggled to make progress.

The swirling current dragged him under and so he pumped his arms and kicked out frantically. After a few worrying moments, his head broke above the surface, but water still poured into his mouth and filled his eyes making him cough and blurring his vision.

He flicked his head and that made the wagon come into focus. Elmina was leaning over the side and when she saw him she thrust out a hand.

Jim took a deep breath and lunged forward. He made slow progress and every movement he made seemed only to splash water rather than moving him forward forcing Elmina to lean further out of the wagon.

He stopped trying to move so he could work out how to get closer to her and almost as if his struggling had been working against him, he drifted closer to the wagon. He raised a hand and it brushed against wood, but he couldn't find purchase and the current again dragged him under.

This time, everything went dark and he feared he'd slipped under the wagon. Then something brushed his fingertips and a hand closed around his right wrist, yanking him to a halt.

He brought his left hand up and a second hand locked around that wrist, too. Elmina tugged and he came up pressed against the side of the wagon.

He shot her a thankful look, but she returned a worried one and so accepting she wasn't strong enough to haul him out, he freed his right hand and grabbed the side. When he felt secure, he drew

127

himself higher.

With her grabbing the back of his jacket and with him scrambling his knees and then feet against the side of the wagon, he came clear of the water. Then, with a relieved sigh, he rolled over the sideboard to land on his back on the wagon.

'Obliged,' he said before getting to his knees and bending over to cough up water.

'That's the way to save someone,' she said. 'Remember that.'

He contented himself with a nod before raising his head to see how close the approaching deluge was. To his surprise, he couldn't see it and even when he got to his feet, all he could see behind them was an even flow of water.

He turned and downstream the creek was churning, while what looked like elongated mounds of water appeared on either side of the wagon. They couldn't be mounds and so after staring at them, he reckoned the water that had been hurtling towards them was now being channelled into the creek.

'The deluge petered out, then?' he asked.

'No,' she said. 'I reckon it slipped underneath us and now we're riding it.'

Jim moved gingerly around the wagon as he got used to the way it pitched on the water. From what he could see, Elmina had understood the situation and while they'd been in the water, the leading edge of the deluge had passed by.

The creek was roiling on either side, but the wagon had settled into travelling down a relatively quieter section of the current. Aside from turning slowly, the wagon was robust enough to be unaffected by the water, leading to Jim slapping the tailboard in triumph.

Elmina directed a beaming smile at him after which they sat down on either side of the wagon to watch out for trouble.

The wagon continued its slow circling and by the time it was again facing downstream, the mounds of water had flattened out leaving the creek brimming over the banks although most of the flow was contained.

With the land to the side relatively free of water, Jim looked for Winslow and his men. The land behind them was free of movement, although ahead a group of riders was facing up the slope.

The wagon was now around a mile from the lake and the group was moving away from it. They had stopped, presumably in concern about the wildness of the creek.

With the water level still in danger of rising high enough to sweep these men away, Jim put his hands around his mouth as he prepared to shout a warning to them. Then he discerned who they were and he barked out a laugh, making Elmina look at him oddly until she noticed what had amused him.

'Pierre Dulaine is on my trail again,' Jim said happily. 'That almost makes me wish the flood had been stronger.'

'Stop gloating and get down,' Elmina said. 'He might see us.'

'That's a good point.'

Jim ducked down slightly, but he ensured he could still watch Pierre. When the wagon was level with him, he braced his feet on the base and stood up.

He waited until Pierre turned to the wagon and although he was too far away to see if his expression was shocked, Jim favoured him with a wave.

Elmina sighed, but then she got into the spirit of the situation and stood up to wave at Pierre, too.

Pierre set his hands on his hips as he watched the wagon sail on by and with him following its progress, Jim removed his hat and provided a deep bow. Then, cheered by the encounter, he turned his attention to the approaching lake.

The creek became wider further on as the slope became less steep and so now he could see only a portion of the lake, while Pegasus Heights was no longer visible.

He wondered if the outcrop had been submerged and so he strained his neck to look out for it, hoping he could confirm his theory about how the wagons had ended up on the summit.

They were still travelling quickly and so within a minute the wagon came surging out of the creek and, on passing a high headland, the outcrop became visible.

Unfortunately, the rock looked to be the same height as it had been when he'd rowed out to it yesterday. Then, without any intervention from him or Elmina, the current carried the wagon on towards Pegasus Heights.

He stood up to consider the outcrop ahead and then the creek behind him. The water was choppy, but it wasn't as wild as it had been, while Pegasus Heights loomed over them.

He judged that even if the deluge from the dam had been a dozen times stronger, it still wouldn't have raised the water level high enough to beach them on the summit.

Elmina watched his behaviour with a bemused expression until with a smile she appeared to pick up on his thoughts.

'What was that theory you were talking about back when we were standing on the dam?' she said.

'I said that we'd beach on Pegasus Heights,' he said. He paused while the wagon moved on until it nudged against the outcrop and ground to a halt. 'And we have.'

CHAPTER 17

'I've told you all before,' Pierre said. 'I'm not following two steps behind Jim Dragon.'

'Forget about him,' Nicholson said. 'Elmina Fay was with him and so clearly they've escaped from Winslow Scott.'

'If that man can rescue her, it suggests he's not the key to what's happening out here.'

Pierre considered Nicholson with triumph as he regained some of his usual confidence. Nicholson couldn't find an answer, but he didn't need to when Grantham pointed up the slope.

'Perhaps you should ask Winslow,' he said. 'He's chasing after the wagon.'

Sure enough, Winslow was leading a group of a dozen men towards them. They were afoot, bedraggled, and plodding along in a weary manner, although when they saw Pierre, Winslow drew them together after which they moved on more purposefully.

'We've seen Elmina,' Pierre called when Winslow

was still fifty feet away. He gestured over his shoulder indicating the lake. 'Jim Dragon was with her.'

Winslow didn't reply immediately as he walked on down the slope and so Pierre dismounted to greet him, encouraging the others to follow his lead.

'And you didn't stop them?' Winslow asked when he reached them.

'They were sailing along in the water, so it wasn't possible for me to . . .' Pierre trailed off when he noted Winslow had directed his question to Murdock.

'Pierre's in charge of this group,' Murdock said. 'I did what he told me to do. So their getting away was his fault.'

His statement rendered Pierre speechless, but Nicholson was already wary of the possibility that Murdock would make his loyalties clear now that they were with Winslow and so he edged closer to Grantham.

'I'm sure it was, but Elmina didn't appear to know anything useful,' Winslow said.

'She might not, but I reckon Jim Dragon does.'

'Why?'

Murdock gestured at Pierre. 'Because this one is always two steps behind him.'

Pierre finally found his voice with a cry of anguish before he pointed at Murdock.

'I hired you for this mission. I won't stand by and let you insult me.'

Murdock shrugged. 'Winslow hired me first.'

He waited until that information had made Pierre

bristle with indignation before he looked at Winslow, who drew his gun.

When this encouraged his men to level guns on Pierre, Nicholson reckoned he'd seen enough, and so before Murdock turned his attention on to them, he backed out of sight behind Pierre's men.

Grantham joined him and with Nicholson judging they would be noticed if they tried to mount their horses, they continued to back away. Nicholson hoped they could duck down behind cover and then use the contours of the slope to find somewhere to hide.

Sure enough, with Pierre demanding an explanation and with Winslow gloating over his answer, they reached a boulder without attracting anyone's interest. The moment they'd slipped behind cover, they stopped being cautious about their retreat and broke into a run.

They'd covered around fifty paces when raised voices sounded behind them. Nicholson looked over his shoulder and when the scene beyond the boulder came into view, Pierre and Winslow were arguing.

As nobody was watching them run away, Nicholson put them from his mind and hurried on. They'd run on for another minute when a gunshot sounded.

Nicholson tried to ignore the sound, but when another shot blasted Grantham looked back, and Nicholson joined him in looking. Winslow's men had fired high and they were hooting at Pierre in derision.

For his part, Pierre was hurrying to his horse. Only

Murdock wasn't watching the altercation, he was peering down the slope at them, seemingly only now noticing that they had fled.

'Keep running,' Grantham said.

'Where to?' Nicholson said.

'Jim Dragon must have ended up somewhere. We might be able to make a stand with him.'

Nicholson agreed with this sentiment and he looked ahead at the lake. They were a half-mile away from the water's edge, but he could see no sign of Jim.

They ran on and they were approaching the lake by the time hoofbeats sounded behind them. Pierre was peering ahead as if searching for where Jim had gone while Winslow was in steady pursuit on one of the horses with the rest of his men trailing behind on foot.

When they reached the lake, they pounded along until they reached the spot where they'd rested up last night. The raft Pierre had used was still beached in the shallows and so they wasted no time clambering aboard.

'All we need to do is put distance between us and Pierre,' Nicholson said as he used a branch to lever them into motion.

'That might not be so easy.' Grantham pointed, 'Pierre reckons we've had the right idea.'

Behind him, Nicholson heard Pierre dismounting and so he concentrated on moving the raft, but it was slow to get started and by the time it was sliding through the water, Pierre was leading his men into the shallows.

'If you get on board, too, you'll capsize us,' Nicholson shouted.

'Drowning is preferable to being shot up,' Pierre said. 'As you'll find out if you don't help me aboard.'

Nicholson ignored him and he continued to shove them out on to the water, leaving Grantham to get Pierre on to the raft. Then the rest of his men followed and took up positions that kept it balanced.

They'd cleared the shallows when Winslow drew up at the side. By the time his men caught up with him, the raft was swinging round to follow the current in the lake.

With a few terse orders Winslow lined his men up at the edge of the water.

Nicholson shouted out a warning a moment before the men started firing. Unlike back up the slope, this time they had targets in mind.

The first volley sliced uselessly into the water ten feet short of the raft, but that just let the men get them in their sights. While Pierre's men were still scrambling for their guns, they fired again.

One man on the raft cried out, his hand rising to clutch his ribs before he keeled over into the water while a second man got a bullet in the neck that made him flop down lifelessly on the raft.

The rest responded in kind and they laid down a sustained burst of gunfire.

With the raft bucking on the choppy water, Nicholson could see that aiming was difficult and so they concentrated on firing quickly. Nicholson didn't

see anyone else go down, but their shooting was fero-
cious enough to worry the gunmen into hurrying for
cover.

By the time Winslow's men had dropped down
behind beached logs and rocks, Nicholson's paddling had moved the raft out into the lake. So their
next volley cut into the water dozens of yards short
and so Pierre ordered his men not to return fire.

The shadow of Pegasus Heights loomed over the
raft making Nicholson note where they were heading
for the first time. He didn't figure he could avoid the
outcrop and so he stopped paddling letting the raft
drift on until it thudded into rock.

'Where now?' he asked Pierre.

'We stay on Pegasus Heights,' Pierre said.

'Why?'

Pierre gave no reply besides looking up at the
outcrop and, after a few moments, Jim Dragon
stepped into view. Jim peered down at the raft considering their predicament with a smile on his face.

'Welcome to my island, Pierre,' he said. 'I hope
you enjoy your stay.'

CHAPTER 18

It was mid-afternoon before Winslow organized his men to head across to Pegasus Heights.

While Jim and Pierre waited for him to make his move, the seriousness of the situation ensured they didn't trade insults and taunts as they usually did.

Instead, Jim and Elmina sat beside the wagon, while Pierre and his surviving men sat facing Winslow's men over the stretch of water.

The collapse of his theory about how the wagon had ended up here had depressed Jim almost as much as Pierre's arrival and the way it'd drawn Winslow to them had.

He tried to cheer himself up by wandering around the wagon and examining it from all angles. When Pierre started murmuring in discontent about Winslow, Elmina joined him.

'What are you doing now?' she asked, her concerned tone showing that she, too, was trying to take her mind off Winslow's imminent arrival.

'I'm trying to come up with an alternate theory

about how the wagon came to be here,' Jim said.

'As Archibald told you, a flying horse flew—'

'I'd prefer a theory that doesn't involve Pegasus.'

'Then you'll struggle.'

Jim let Elmina have the last word and he looked again at the creek that led up to the loggers' camp. It wasn't the only source of water for the lake, but it would take a massive increase in the volume of water to strand the wagon up here naturally.

As the wagon getting here accidentally was unlikely, the only other option was that someone had brought it here deliberately.

With Pierre studiously avoiding looking at him, the thought came that he had often played tricks on Pierre and he'd fooled him every time, but he wasn't the only one who could play tricks.

He moved back to the wagon, his furrowed brow making Elmina watch him carefully. Experimentally, he pushed the wagon.

The wheels wouldn't turn and instead the structure rocked back and forth while rattling so loudly it looked in danger of collapsing. The noise made Pierre look at him for the first time in a while.

'Your nemesis is about to arrive and kill us all,' he said. 'And yet you're wasting your time playing with that rickety wagon.'

'I had always thought that you considered yourself to be my nemesis.'

'I consider that you are my nemesis, but my point is that the wagon you sailed to reach here has now drifted back to the side, and Winslow intends to use it to come over here. So forget about that wagon.'

'And my point is that Winslow suspects that Elmina knows something about Chadwick Jackson and his raids, and about Igor Rodgers and the missing supplies, but he could have left Marshal Collier to investigate. So he has no reason to want you dead, other than the pleasure I'm sure anyone would get from killing you.'

Pierre conceded his taunt with a curt nod before he turned to two of his men, Nicholson and Grantham.

'And Murdock was working for Winslow, too,' Pierre said. 'He turned on me.'

'As Jim Dragon said, that's hardly surprising,' Nicholson said, making Jim smile and Pierre scowl. 'But Murdock had something else in mind. He reckoned Jim could lead Winslow to a large prize.'

This revelation made Elmina step forward and catch Jim's eye, but Pierre didn't notice.

'And yet he's determined to eliminate us and we don't know nothing about this larger prize.' Pierre turned to Jim and Jim nodded as they both came to the same conclusion. 'Unless Winslow's not concerned about us, only this place.'

'This outcrop is barren,' Elmina said. 'There's nothing on it except for this abandoned wagon, and there's nothing on the wagon.'

They stood in silence for a while until Richard attracted Pierre's attention.

'Winslow's got himself organized,' he said. 'They're all coming over.'

Pierre hurried over to the edge of the outcrop. What he saw below made him wince and so, despite feeling that the answer was close, Jim moved to join him.

Elmina took his arm and stopped him.

'I hired you for a reason,' she said. 'I may call you an idiot, but I know you're the man who can find Pegasus.'

When she released his arm, Jim glanced again at the wagon.

If he wanted to keep someone away from somewhere, ignoring that place would usually work, but when dealing with a suspicious mind, drawing attention to the place might make someone look elsewhere.

'The wagon's not important,' he said. 'The important point is that it's fragile, and that's because someone dismantled it, brought the parts up here, and then reassembled them.'

She frowned. 'It's possible, but why?'

'It's a distraction to make some people think about a silly local legend concerning a flying horse and make other people like us waste time trying to work out how it got up here. That would stop us spending time thinking about the real mystery of who really killed Igor Rodgers. And that's the same piece of deception that was carried out ten years ago to stop people working out who killed the gold prospector.'

She shrugged. 'I like that you're thinking at last, but even if you're right, it doesn't help us.'

141

'It does, because that means whoever went to all the effort of getting the wagon up here is the same person who had the idea of placing a wagon here ten years ago.'

Elmina raised an eyebrow and then put a relieved hand to her heart when she picked up on the full implication of his theory.

'My father was here ten years ago with Winslow Scott, but only Winslow is here now.'

Jim nodded, although he wasn't sure where that thought led him. So he joined everyone in standing on the edge of the outcrop.

Another wagon was below, sailing out on to the lake. This one was full of gunmen, and they'd reach the outcrop within a few minutes.

CHAPTER 19

Gunfire blasted as Pierre's men fired down at the wagon. Then retaliatory gunfire tore out and hammered into rock forcing them to dive aside.

As he'd lost his gun in the water, Jim didn't want to stray towards the edge and so he hurried back to the wagon, figuring he had a better use for it than letting it stand there taunting him.

He stood at the back. Then, more forcefully than before, he pushed.

The wheels had locked solidly and so the wagon skidded along the summit. After covering only a few feet, his strength gave out and the wagon shuddered to a halt, but Nicholson and Grantham saw what he was trying to do and they joined him in standing at the back.

'Winslow and Murdock will be here in a minute,' Nicholson said, pointing at the area they needed to aim for to hit the men below.

'He expects gunfire,' Grantham said with a grin. 'He won't expect a huge wagon landing on his head.'

They shoved and even though the wheels stayed locked, the wagon screeched along the summit. Pierre and his men shot bemused looks at them, but they didn't complain as the front of the wagon reached them.

When the front end protruded over the edge, Elmina joined them and peered down to check on Winslow's position below. With gestures she urgently hurried them on while ordering them to move the wagon to the right.

They stopped pushing and congregated at the left-hand corner, but the moment the wagon settled back in place it creaked ominously. Then it collapsed.

The wheels splayed sideways depositing the wagon on the ground and then the backs and sides toppled away making everyone jump aside.

With the wagon being close to the edge, the front end rocked down and then up over clear space before it slid out of view, taking most of the structure with it.

In fragments, the wagon along with three of the wheels toppled over the side, and the cries of alarm from below suggested the broken wagon was harder to avoid than the intact one would have been.

As Nicholson and Grantham hurled wood over the side, Jim looked down. Below, the debris had knocked two men into the water.

With other men cringing to avoid the debris that Nicholson and Grantham launched over the edge, Winslow's men laid down a burst of gunfire that forced them to seek cover amongst the rocks.

'You seem to make a habit of making a mess of things and yet they still work out,' Elmina said at his shoulder.

'That's how I got my reputation as a winner.' Jim fingered his lucky shark's tooth until she smiled. Then he pointed at the remnants of the wagon. 'And the wagon fell apart so readily I reckon I've proved Winslow had it dismantled and reassembled up here, both now and ten years ago.'

'I congratulate you. Now, where's Pegasus?'

Jim frowned, but he didn't explain any more of his thoughts on the matter when he saw Murdock rootling through the debris. Before Jim could work out what he was looking for, Winslow ordered his men to fire back.

Lead sliced into the edge of the outcrop forcing Jim to back away and, after a few more shots, the rest of the defenders moved out of sight.

Silence reigned for a minute, but when Pierre glanced over the edge, three shots tore out forcing him back.

'We re-group over there,' he said, gathering his men around him. 'We let them come to us and then we make them pay.'

His three men lined up, but Nicholson and Grantham joined Jim instead.

'I saw what Murdock was doing, too,' Nicholson said. 'He knows that there's something worth finding here.'

'And he seems to think it's on the wagon,' Jim said.

Both men nodded and so he hurried along the summit to get to the side of Winslow's men. He looked down cautiously.

Five gunmen led by Winslow were ten yards from the summit planning their move on to the top, but Murdock was trying to rescue an innocuous looking plank from the water.

Jim beckoned Elmina to stay up on the top, but she shook her head.

'Nowhere is safe,' she said. 'And I want answers.'

Jim nodded and picked out a route down the side of the outcrop that avoided the gunmen while staying out of Murdock's line of sight. With Jim leading, they snaked downwards.

By the time they were skirting along the water's edge, Winslow's men were lying just beneath the edge. Then Winslow waved ahead and the men swarmed on to the top and out of sight.

Gunfire erupted as they took on Pierre's men, while Murdock lunged for the plank and hoisted it out of the water before he looked up. The fact that both sets of gunmen would be fighting for their lives didn't appear to concern him and he peered at the plank.

Jim worked his way closer as Murdock turned the wood over in his hands. He got to within four feet of him when, with a sudden movement, Murdock looked up at him and then swung the plank back-handed.

Jim saw the wood coming and he jerked aside, but Grantham and Nicholson were at his heels and they

146

didn't see what Murdock was doing until the last moment. The heavy plank slammed into Grantham's left shoulder knocking him aside so strongly his feet left the ground.

Nicholson was standing higher up than Grantham was and the plank caught him with a glancing blow to the chest that made him fold over before he stumbled backwards.

Elmina moved to stop him falling over, but on the slippery rocks she succeeded only in tipping herself over.

Murdock surveyed the effect of his first swing with a grin and swung the plank up on to a shoulder. With a huge step forward he brushed Jim aside with a meaty fist that knocked him backwards until he slammed up against the outcrop.

Then he stood over Grantham and raised the wood high above his head ready to dash it down on his head.

Grantham rolled over on to his back to look up at Murdock. With only moments to act, Jim kicked out and slammed the heel of his boot into Murdock's calf.

The blow wasn't powerful enough to upend him, but on the slippery rocks Murdock had to shift his weight as he swung the plank down.Grantham anticipated where the plank would land and he rolled to the right as the wood crashed down on to rock sending up a flurry of splinters and shards of broken wood.

Murdock grunted in anger as he tossed the shortened length of wood away before lunging down and

147

grabbing Grantham's jacket front in one hand. Then he raised Grantham off the ground.

Grantham battered at his hand without effect and so while Nicholson moved in on him, Jim clambered on to a boulder and leapt on Murdock's back.

Aside from setting his feet wide apart, Murdock didn't register that Jim was causing him any problems and so Jim wrapped a hand around his chin.

Jim drew back, but he couldn't move Murdock's head and without any apparent difficulty, Murdock swung back a fist as he prepared to punch Grantham.

Nicholson saw what Murdock intended to do and with a shake of the head he leapt to his feet. As quickly as he was able to, he charged Murdock, going in low and slapping his shoulders into Murdock's stomach.

Murdock teetered, but even with three people manhandling him, he still thudded a fierce punch into Grantham's cheek that cracked his head back. Murdock punched him a second time with a back-handed swipe, but then, almost as if he'd noticed the other men for the first time, he glanced down at Nicholson and smiled.

He slapped his hand over Jim's hand and squeezed. Jim screeched and with his fingers going numb, he couldn't keep his hold and he slipped off Murdock's back.

While Murdock shook Nicholson aside with ease, Jim nursed his hand. He was still wondering how he could take Murdock on when Murdock delivered his fiercest blow so far by thudding an uppercut into

Grantham's jaw.

The punch tore Grantham away from Murdock's grasp and sent him falling backwards for several feet until he thudded down on his back.

'At my feet, as I wanted,' Murdock said happily. 'Now it's your time to die.'

He rolled his shoulders making Jim catch Nicholson's eye so they could co-ordinate an assault, even though the effort felt futile. Nicholson was looking up the slope and, when he noticed Jim's interest, he waved at him to back away before leaping aside.

Jim had no intention of giving up and he rocked his weight down on his toes ready to spring forward, but then he heard a rumble.

At first, he assumed that the gunfire up on the summit had grown in intensity, but then, from the corner of his eye, he saw movement. Even though he couldn't work out what it was, on instinct he followed Nicholson's lead and leapt aside.

He landed on his chest in a pool of water where he shook himself. Then he turned to find rocks rolling closer as a veritable landslide thundered down the slope.

He scrambled backwards as one rock skimmed past his leg while another headed for his chest.

He couldn't avoid the rock, but at the last moment it took a fortuitous deflection and skidded over his form. He looked for more falling rocks and although he could see mainly dust, one large rock crunched down before Murdock and then slammed into his chest.

With a pained cry Murdock toppled over backwards and slipped from view. A moment later, two loud splashes sounded.

Jim waited until the dust started settling and he was sure that the landslide had ended before he got up. Murdock wasn't visible, but Grantham and Nicholson were both lying on their backs.

They were groaning, seemingly having failed to avoid all of the rocks, but they were moving and so Jim judged they hadn't been badly injured.

He couldn't see Elmina either and with the gunfire still rattling away on the summit, with mounting trepidation he clambered on to a boulder.

'Over here,' Elmina called, her voice coming from high up on Pegasus Heights and behind him.

He turned and he couldn't help but laugh when he saw she was leaning on a short plank while sporting a triumphant smile.

'Did you cause the landslide?' he asked.

'Sure.' She patted the plank. 'You all looked like you needed rescuing.'

Jim conceded her success with a bow before he moved to where Murdock had been standing. Ripples were still spreading out from where he'd landed in the water, but he couldn't see him.

As he then noticed that the gunfire had stopped, he figured he had enough time to try to work out what Murdock had been doing.

The plank that Murdock had been examining and which he'd used as a weapon was lying at Jim's feet. The only feature on it was the emblem of the Pegasus

Lumber Company, its dark form having been chipped by Murdock's actions.

Jim followed Murdock's lead and examined the plank. What he saw made him raise an eyebrow.

Then, before anyone noticed his interest, he moved on and joined Nicholson, who was rubbing a bruised leg.

Grantham had come out of the crisis the worst and aside from the punches he'd received, he was holding his hip while sporting a pained expression.

Jim motioned Nicholson to take care of him before moving on up the slope. When he joined Elmina, she'd already lost her good humour.

From higher up, Jim could see why. Murdock's body was floating off with his head down in the water.

'You did what you had to do,' Jim said.

'I know, but the truth about Pegasus probably died with him,' she said.

With her looking distraught, Jim reckoned that he didn't need to order her to stay here. It had been ominously quiet on the summit for the last few minutes and so he moved on.

As Winslow's men had done, he paused before he reached the top and tentatively looked over the edge before ducking back down. He shot a worried glance at Elmina before shuffling along to one of the men who had been shot earlier.

He claimed a gun off him and then considered the scene again.

Several men had gone down in the gunfight that had raged on the summit. Only three men had survived the battle and now Winslow and one other man was holding Pierre at gunpoint.

Pierre had his hands raised while the two men's attention was on him.

'Where is it?' Winslow said.

'You have to believe me when I say that I don't know what you're searching for,' Pierre said. 'Perhaps if we were to sit down and discuss—'

'Talk or die!' Winslow spat.

As talking was the only skill Pierre had and that had failed, Jim sighed to himself. Then, against his better judgement, he stood up.

'Perhaps you should talk to me about the flying horse instead,' he said.

CHAPTER 20

'Drop the gun and then join Pierre,' Winslow said, gesturing with his gun.

Jim moved on to the summit and with his gun held low, he stood ten feet to Pierre's left facing Winslow and the other man.

'I defeated Murdock,' Jim said. 'He's floating away face down in the water. If you don't want to join him, drop your gun.'

'Leave this to me, Monsieur Dragon,' Pierre said before Winslow could retort. 'Before you arrived I was dealing with the situation without any need for unsavoury threats.'

'You were about to get shot up!'

'I'd already ascertained that these gentlemen want something, and when men want something, Pierre Dulaine can always provide it.'

Pierre favoured Jim with a withering look before turning back to Winslow, who considered him with an equally irritated expression.

'You two will stop arguing and explain yourself,'

Winslow muttered.

Pierre waved his arms above his head, conveying his own exasperation before pointing at Winslow.

'That is what I'm trying to do, and now I'll explain everything.'

Pierre smiled. Then a gunshot popped, the sound surprising Jim as neither gunman appeared to have fired.

Only when Winslow staggered backwards clutching his chest did Jim work out what had happened, but by then Pierre had swung his arm to the left and with a flick of his forearm, he shot the second gunman.

Pierre watched both men keel over backwards. When they hit the ground and they both didn't move again, he turned to Jim and smiled.

Then Pierre showed him the small, concealed pistol that nestled on his palm. He shrugged his arm and the pistol disappeared up his sleeve.

'I believe you may have learnt a few things from me about deception,' Jim said.

Pierre delivered a short bow. 'And for once I welcomed one of your famous distractions.'

Pierre then moved away. Jim still watched him to ensure he wouldn't turn the gun on him, but Pierre looked over the edge of the outcrop with concern before moving out of view.

Jim followed him. Below, Elmina was looking up and so Jim nodded to her before working his way down to help Nicholson and Grantham get back up to the summit.

While Pierre examined the bodies of his fallen men, they climbed up without too much difficulty and when they joined him on the top, Grantham reported he'd been bruised, but he had no broken bones.

As they were the only survivors, they settled down amidst the remaining debris from the collapsed wagon to work out what they did next.

'Clearly Murdock was convinced that something was up here,' Nicholson said. 'But I doubt we'll find it now.'

'I'd settle for leaving this place and never returning,' Grantham said while ruefully rubbing his ribs.

'So would I,' Elmina said. She considered Winslow's body and sighed before placing her hands on her hips. 'But after all the trouble, I'm not leaving with nothing.'

Jim nodded, but he didn't offer an opinion and instead, he moved away to look over the edge of the rock.

Pierre was no longer checking on the dead men, and Jim couldn't see him even when he peered as far over the edge as he dared.

Fearing the worst, he moved to the side until movement behind a higher stretch of rock caught his attention. Worse, the movement was out on the water.

He hurried along until he saw that the wagon Winslow had used to reach the outcrop was now drifting away from them with Pierre sitting on the back. He was letting the current guide him, but based on his own experiences, Jim reckoned that before long it would take him to the side of the lake.

As this the only way off the outcrop, Jim shook a fist at him until Pierre looked up.

'It seems I will get to return to Beaver Ridge first to explain everything to Marshal Collier,' Pierre called. 'Then, while I enjoy my bones, you can enjoy yourself sitting on that big rock as you await a rescue that may or may not come.'

'Enjoy your temporary victory, Pierre, because I'll get my bones back,' Jim shouted, his comment making the others hurry over to see what had concerned him.

'You'll fail, as you have failed here.' Pierre waved to him. 'And now, I'll bid you a less than fond *adieu.*'

'And I'll bid you a less than fond *au revoir.*'

Pierre shrugged. '*Adieu* means goodbye. *Au revoir* means we will meet again.'

Jim felt his shark's tooth and then nodded.

'I know that.'

Pierre returned the nod. 'In that case, *au revoir* it is, *Monsieur* Dragon.'

'So it looks like we'll be here all night and maybe even longer,' Nicholson said as the sun dipped below the nearby hills.

Grantham nodded. 'Some wood is sure to beach up here eventually, but if it doesn't, I reckon I'll be strong enough tomorrow to swim away.'

Nicholson looked at Jim and Elmina, presumably for their opinion. Since Pierre had abandoned them, they'd been quiet, the trauma of the gunfight and the line of bodies lying further along the outcrop depressing them all.

Even though Elmina appeared glum, Jim watched the sunset with a smile on his face.

'I'm sure we'll be able to leave soon,' he said.

He looked at Elmina, expecting the usual sarcastic reaction, but she shrugged.

'We will, but I can't see why you're so content. Pierre will get to Beaver Ridge first and he'll be able to tell Marshal Collier what happened out here. He was right that the marshal will be so grateful he'll give him your bones.'

'Maybe I have other things on my mind.' Jim looked again at the sun until it brushed the hills. 'I gather the last flying horse to come here arrived at sundown.'

She stared at him with bemusement while Nicholson and Grantham laughed.

'Did you bang your head earlier?' she asked.

'No. I'm pleased to hear you no longer believe the story, but I do now. The flying horse Pegasus will come and it will solve all our problems. I reckon sundown is the right time.'

'Why at sundown?'

'Well, it doesn't have to be then, but I figure that'll give Pierre enough time to get well away from here.'

'I guess the sight of Pegasus flapping its way across the lake might surprise him.' Elmina snorted a laugh and then gestured at the sun. 'But it's close to sundown now and I don't see no flying horse.'

Jim got to his feet and moved over to the debris of the wagon that had stayed on the summit. One of the sides was intact and he picked it up and brought it back to the group.

In the centre of the wood was the carved emblem of the Pegasus Lumber Company, which he showed to them. Then he waited for one of them to hazard a guess.

'Are you saying we lash this wood together and build a raft?' Nicholson said.

'I don't reckon it's strong enough, but if some more debris from the dam washes up here, it might prove useful.' Jim tapped the emblem. 'And we'll have this flying horse to help us.'

They all shrugged and so he stroked the emblem and then turned over the wood. Thick tar had been used to hold the carving in place and it had cracked.

He had to scrape at the tar with a stone to remove a section, and beneath was a metal that gleamed.

Better still, his actions broke the wood and the carving detached itself and landed on the ground with a dull clunk. He picked it up, letting everyone see that the wood carving was hollow and that inside was the flat, golden statue of a flying horse.

'Pegasus,' Elmina said with delight, while Nicholson and Grantham looked the emblem over with surprise. 'Igor Rodgers did find the horse and he escaped with it, after all. Then he hid it so well nobody could find it until you did.'

'I can't take all the credit,' Jim said. 'Murdock was fighting with a section of the plank that contained the emblem from the other side of the wagon. But he'd found the carving from the wrong side of the wagon and that one was entirely wooden.'

While Nicholson nodded, Jim held out the golden horse to Elmina.

'I believe this is yours,' he said. 'It might not be capable of flying away, but then again, I never expected to find a live flying horse.'

'Maybe not, but I'll settle for owning a golden one.' She shrugged. 'And for knowing that Winslow Scott was behind everything that happened here ten years ago and not my father.'

'Then I've completed your quest to your satisfaction, as I always knew I would.'

'As did I.'

She favoured him with a wink and a beaming smile before she turned to look towards Beaver Ridge.

Jim joined her in looking that way as he put his mind to how he would get off the outcrop, catch up with Pierre, and then get his bones back.

This time, he didn't feel a need to finger his shark's tooth.

WESTMEATH COUNTY LIBRARY

3 0019 00425028 2